WORDS AREN'T NECESSARY

He took another step. "I would do anything in my power for you. I want you to know this. I have never known a woman stronger, more generous, more compassionate than you—or to whom I owe so much."

She gulped. From somewhere she drew strength from sheer force of will.

"You—you are mistaken. I am not so . . . not so—"

He closed the gap between them. There was no more moonlight, only his enveloping shadow, and he reached down and took her arms, drawing her up.

"You must not say—" she began.

"Hush."

"—any more."

That was when his arms slipped around her shoulders, and his soft lips brushed her hair.

"Annabelle . . ."

He kissed her hair. He brushed a soft feathery kiss upon her brow. And then he pulled her tightly to him and pressed her face close.

"Annabelle, how can I let you go?" he whispered.

SIGNET

REGENCY ROMANCE
COMING IN JUNE 2004

Viscount Vagabond and *The Devil's Delilah*
by Loretta Chase
Now, for the first time, these two wonderful classics
are bound together in one volume!
0-451-21223-1

The Barkin Emeralds
by Nancy Butler
On behalf of her mistress, Miss Maggie Bonner is
returning a rejected betrothal gift to Lord Barkin in
Scotland. But when she is mistaken for his intended,
she is kidnapped by a dashing pirate.
0-451-21175-8

A Worthy Opponent
by Louise Bergin
Miss Judith Shelton is happy to admit that she's a
fortune hunter, but she has her orphaned sibling's best
interests at heart. Judith has no romantic notions of
love—until she meets the cunning friend of the man
whose fortune she's hunting.
0-451-21013-1

Available wherever books are sold, or
to order call: 1-800-788-6262

Deceiving
Miss Dearborn

Laurie Bishop

A SIGNET BOOK

SIGNET
Published by New American Library, a division of
Penguin Group (USA) Inc., 375 Hudson Street,
New York, New York 10014, U.S.A.
Penguin Books Ltd, 80 Strand,
London WC2R 0RL, England
Penguin Books Australia Ltd, 250 Camberwell Road,
Camberwell, Victoria 3124, Australia
Penguin Books Canada Ltd, 10 Alcorn Avenue,
Toronto, Ontario, Canada M4V 3B2
Penguin Books (N.Z.) Ltd, Cnr Rosedale and Airborne Roads,
Albany, Auckland 1310, New Zealand

Penguin Books Ltd, Registered Offices:
80 Strand, London WC2R 0RL, England

First published by Signet, an imprint of New American Library,
a division of Penguin Group (USA) Inc.

First Printing, May 2004
10 9 8 7 6 5 4 3 2 1

To my sister Jennifer,
who wouldn't let me give up
and who saw more possibilities in me
than I did in myself.

Chapter One

*F*rom what he could make out, staring up from the bottom of the deep ditch, it was daylight. It also looked like rain.

It looked like rain, and he lay in the roadside ditch as naked as the day he was born.

He couldn't remember anything. Not where he was, not why he was there . . . and not who he was.

He was a mystery to himself.

Naked!

He knew just one thing. Whoever he was, he wouldn't ordinarily be naked in a public ditch . . . or a private ditch, for that matter.

He wondered if he'd had a cup too much. Slowly he began to search his mouth for a hint of aftertaste. He only encountered two things: pain and blood.

He had either had a bad accident, or someone had beaten him senseless.

He drew in a breath, slowly, and experienced the motley stabs and aches as the air filled his lungs. There were so many tender and painful spots, they ran together and blurred into one, making him one hurting and sorry fellow.

He blinked his swollen eyelids and stared at the

strip of sky. Damme. He doubted hell was this good—
or purgatory this bad—so he was still living the life
he hadn't the faintest memory of.

He must be a man of a practical, stubborn disposi-
tion, for he recognized the need to move, to get up, to
go somewhere else. It was not good to lie in a ditch
ass bare and stare at what one supposed to be the sky,
which became grayer as he watched, while one decided if one were a drunk or a fool.

Sitting up was a challenge and a truly agonizing experience that he wished would go the way of the rest
of his memories. When he had accomplished this, he
found next to him a gray shapeless lump—some kind
of primitive cloth. No, it was wool, roughly spun and
loomed. Carefully he reached for it, and when he was
able to balance his upper body without the support of
his other arm, he grasped the cloth in two hands and
held it open.

It was a homespun coat—worn, punctuated with
holes, and smelling like all the filthy, unwashed beggars he had ever had the misfortune to pass on the
street.

What street? Where? He didn't seem to be in a city.
This was a country road, he was sure, and no carriage
or cart or rider or pedestrian had passed since he had
forced his eyes open.

It was gone then, the smoky image he grappled for.
The only faint surety he retained was that when he
had encountered the beggars somewhere in his past,
he had been fully clothed, and he had . . . scorned
them. Scorned them? Pitied them? He wasn't sure but
for the fact that he had not been a beggar himself.

That left a very wide field of possibilities.

Alternately wincing, stiffening with pain, and holding his breath to squelch a gasp or a yelp, he slipped

his arms into the smelly coat. It was more than big enough, and since he was no small man, it had previously been worn by one well-fed beggar. He was thankful for that, for he could wrap it securely around himself. If he could find something that could serve as a belt, he could walk—or stumble—without concern that he would provide an impromptu peep show to an unsuspecting passerby.

The light was fading, and a damp wind began to stir. He shuddered. He could delay it no longer. By painful inches, he crawled up the bank to the edge of the rolling field beside the road and collapsed.

A few moments passed. He felt the cooling of the breeze. At last he forced himself up on his hands and knees.

He saw no one in his limited field of vision, as his neck was too stiff to turn very far and his eyelids too swollen to decipher much if it could. Using all his will, he found his feet. Hunched with pain, stiff, and befuddled, he turned slowly, gazing around himself.

English countryside. He was certain of that. Thank God there was another thing he was certain of! The next thing he was equally sure of was that he needed shelter, and he needed food. Instinct told him that neither would be his for the asking, although his gut told him this was wrong. He should not feel so helpless. He should not feel so alone.

Matters, however, were not normal. He would follow his instincts, for they seemed better tuned to the strange world he found himself inhabiting.

The nameless man began to walk, having not the slightest idea where he was going or what he might find beyond the next rise.

*   *   *

She would have to sell Father's ruby ring. She had not wanted to; she had refrained from doing so for too long already. But, heavens, what could she do when there was nothing left to sell?

Miss Annabelle Dearborn slumped in the big oak chair and planted her elbow on the scattered bills and letters of account that littered her desk. Then she rested her chin in the palm of her hand and gazed unseeingly between the faded damask curtains to the gently rolling landscape of Leicestershire. Before her on the mat of bills lay the ring, its red eye glinting in the morning light.

She would have to tell Mother, of course, and Mother would raise a lament, although Mother did not care so very much for the ring—of that, Annabelle was convinced. But Mother would be equally convinced that she *ought* to, and therefore would present an appearance of caring.

Joseph remained silent. Annabelle felt him standing behind her in patient attention, knowing she would respond to his voiced concern in her time. She must respond, for she was the sole mistress of Hartleigh. Joseph, who in his day had been groom, coachman, her father's butler, and now her concierge—in reality, her right hand and advisor for her pretty country inn—knew this. And he also knew the importance of his post in spite of being called by the familiar "Joseph," as the family had always done. Annabelle depended upon him to manage all the things that her sex and station prevented her from doing—she was, in effect, the mistress of Hartleigh, but she clung to appearances still.

Admittedly, appearances were getting near impossible to maintain. She'd had her one and only season before her father had managed to lose all, including her portion and her mother's. Now he was in the hereafter and past worry, while Joseph calmly informed her that the henhouse had been raided again.

"It might be a fox," Annabelle said.

"I am afraid a fox that takes only eggs would be almost as unusual as a fox milking our cows."

"Oh, that is right. You did say that no hens were lost this time." Annabelle sighed. "Perhaps Lizzie made a mistake with the milk yesterday morning. Might she have spilled it? She is such a flighty creature."

"She was very certain that she had not spilled any."

Joseph was convinced that the raider was of the very clever two-legged variety. Annabelle was beginning to believe this, herself. She remembered the tearful milkmaid, Lizzie, asserting that the cows had been partially milked again, before she had touched them.

Of all things Annabelle did not want to believe right now, least of all was that Hartleigh had a thief to add to its growing pile of problems.

"But at least no milk was taken this morning," Annabelle said.

"I am only assuming the cows were untouched. I have heard nothing yet this morning of milk."

"As we are now confining the cows at night, I should think they are safe. No thief would be so brazen as to enter the stable to milk them! Yet entering the henhouse is a bold move indeed. Perhaps Lizzie told the truth yesterday."

"Yes. My thoughts exactly."

Annabelle paused in thought, searching for a remedy, but nothing new occurred to her. "We cannot spare Angus to be on guard all night," Annabelle said, "and we cannot afford to hire another manservant."

"It is indeed a predicament, Miss Dearborn."

"To think I must pay for flour and tea while someone steals my eggs and milk!" Annabelle made a fist on the pile of bills but was too much the lady to pound it on the desktop. "And then there is the expense of wax candles and the need of new linens and Mother's constant use of the apothecary. . . . And I must not forget Madame la Comtesse. Regardless of how foolish you believe I am, I cannot bring myself to turn her out. I am sure she has nowhere else to go."

"I would never think you foolish, Miss Dearborn. You state our financial situation very well." Joseph cleared his throat. "It is unfortunate that our Madame has misplaced her fortune under the circumstances."

She turned her head at last and viewed Joseph, who stood tall and stately in his perennial black suit coat and breeches, his gray hair tied in a neat queue at the back of his neck, his weathered face set in an expression of watchfulness.

"Oh, Joseph! It is an imaginary fortune, as is her title. What difference do the imaginings of an old woman make? They make her content, and she eats very little, after all."

"No difference whatsoever, except when she cannot pay her bed and board. But I do not question your decision, Miss Dearborn. You have always given all matters diligent thought and care."

Annabelle sighed again. "Very well, Joseph. All things being as they may, I suppose what must be addressed at this moment is breakfast. Captain Morgan never says a word, but the others will fuss. Mr. Goodfellow will threaten to take his leave again, I suspect."

She wanted a solution; and she knew very well that Joseph wanted one, too. The fact that he advocated financial discretion confirmed her worst fears. Joseph believed their plight to be as impossible as she did.

"This is so irksome!" she said. "If the stable protects the cows no more than the henhouse protects the hens, the cows might just as well be at pasture all night. I simply cannot think what else to do."

"If I may suggest something, Miss Dearborn."

"Please do."

"I feel we need to employ someone in the capacity of guard, regardless of how impossible that may seem. He need not be expensive; no skill need be expected of him, other than he watches by night. We seem to be at an uncomfortable disadvantage, and it is not only our stock that is at stake. Safety is an issue, and so, of course, is our reputation as an establishment."

Annabelle studied Joseph's quiet face for a moment. "Perhaps you are right." She paused again. "It is becoming very difficult, Joseph."

"I understand. I shall put my mind to the task."

"Thank you. You are very good."

Joseph bowed and let himself out of her small office, leaving Annabelle to stare, deep in thought, out the window at the back garden. Closing her hand around the ruby ring, she caressed its familiar shape with her thumb.

It was Annabelle who cared for the ring. Father had been a failure as a provider, but she had loved him, and he told her the day he had placed the ring in her hand, as he lay in his sickbed, that this was one thing that would be hers forever.

Oh, he had been fantasizing again. As if one ruby ring could make all right! But she had thanked God for his belief then, for it had comforted him, and he had followed his ancestors a fortnight later.

She had found a way, in spite of Mother's protests. She had shepherded their small finances carefully and had converted their family manor into a genteel boarding house, in hopes of capturing the trade of the more fastidious travelers. Situated as they were in Leicestershire off the road leading north, it seemed possible. But hopes had not been fulfilled. Instead, she had only Captain Morgan, Mr. Goodfellow, Madame la Comtesse, and this ring.

"Father," she said then aloud, "if you see any hope for us now, send me a sign." Perhaps from beyond the grave he had gained wisdom.

However, it all must wait. She really did need to go speak to the cook.

Mrs. Bottom, her cook, met her in the hall, apparently intent on seeking her out. Annabelle saw, with growing hopelessness, that Mrs. Bottom was distressed.

"Miss Dearborn, I shall tear my hair out, by the grace of the Lord above! Lizzie will *not* go to the stable this morning. Look at the hour, and the cows are not milked yet! She is convinced the thief is hiding there, waiting to leap upon her! That girl!" Mrs. Bottom waved her wooden spoon emphatically. "I need cream for butter! I cannot be getting it myself!"

Annabelle straightened her shoulders. "No, of course not. You are not expected to."

"That is good," sputtered Mrs. Bottom, "because it isn't worth my wage! Or what I have coming to me, at least!"

Annabelle quelled a shiver of alarm. If Mrs. Bottom were to leave, to be sure, the rest of her small staff would follow . . . except Joseph. But even Joseph had a future to provide for.

Annabelle stiffened her back and brushed by Mrs. Bottom, heading for the service stair. "Do not worry. I shall have matters in hand in very short order. And I shall get your milk."

"Miss?" Mrs. Bottom sounded bewildered. Annabelle started down the narrow stair and heard Mrs. Bottom's determined step behind her.

"Miss, wait!"

Resolved, Annabelle marched into the kitchen, followed by the now-protesting Mrs. Bottom.

"It isn't seemly, Miss! For either you or me, it isn't right! You cannot be going to the stable to milk!"

Annabelle strode through the cavernous kitchen and into the pantry without breaking stride. She swept the pail off the pantry hook. "Oh, but I am. It has to be done. And you are needed right here, while I am not, so it is settled."

Annabelle turned her back on Mrs. Bottom and, continuing her march through the kitchen, snatched a stained apron off the peg by the garden door and stepped out. The fresh breeze of morning swept over her, with its lulling sounds and smells.

From the distance she heard the bells from their flock of sheep going to pasture, a tinkle here, a clink there. The wind brought the faint whistle of the boy who herded them, and the joyful yip of his dog. Her horse, Molly, snorted softly from within her stall. From the distant wood she heard the harsh single call of a raven. And in the wind also came the scent of fresh grass and clover, the sweetness of honeysuckle. It was early still, and the morning light was sharp and clear, tinged with a hint of gold.

Annabelle followed the flagstone path past the kitchen garden and came around the back of the stable, a barren-looking building in sad disrepair.

Only a week ago, when Lizzie reported that the animals were coming dry to the byre, Annabelle had de-

cided that the cows must be brought in at night. Fortunately there had been room for them. Besides the
cows, the stable housed her mare and Mother's, plus
the team of stalwart farm horses—the only remaining
of the full stable that had been Father's pride.

It also had space in the loft for the boy Dick and
Angus to sleep. She had been putting them up in the
attic still, however, because the nights were cool, Dick
was young, and Angus was less likely to discover a
bottle when he slept in the house.

Sleeping in the house did not make Angus more
prompt, however. If it did, he would have done the
stable chores already this morning and allayed
Lizzie's fears.

Annabelle paused as she always did by Molly's
stall. She cooed softly to her mare, and a friendly bay
muzzle extended itself over the half door. Annabelle
stroked the velvet muzzle and gazed into Molly's
beautiful brown eyes.

"Molly, my lovely, did Angus exercise you yesterday? And did you get your fill of clover? How ne-
glectful I have been. I promise we shall ride together
soon."

Molly answered with her soft *phut-phut-phut* sound,
then gently lipped Annabelle's hand.

"I forgot," Annabelle said mournfully. "I shall come
back tonight with a treat. Now I must milk Elizabeth,
Mary, and Therese, and then you shall all be let out to
pasture for some very nice grass."

Annabelle went to the first stall and slipped inside,
secured a rope to Elizabeth's halter, and led her out
onto the brick floor of the stable where it was clean. In
a moment she had Elizabeth tied securely, then pulled
up the small milking stool. Lastly, she hitched up her

long skirt and secured it with her apron so it would
not trail in the straw.

"Behave, now. I know you are not used to me, but
neither am I used to you."

It was odd to consider that she had any experience
at all in milking a cow. She had not had until after her
father's death, when the influenza had gone through
the household, and the first time had been both intim-
idating and distressing. *To think that I have come to this*,
she had thought then. She'd had her come-out at
eighteen but had become a milkmaid at twenty! Now
she was twenty-two, and her fortune had not
changed.

Annabelle closed the door on the painful thoughts
that battered against it. One did as one must.

She sat on the stool, leaned close to the cow's
udder, grasped Elizabeth's near teats, and began the
task, smelling the pungent aroma of cow and fresh
milk. The streams of milk played a rhythmic tune on
the bottom of the empty pail.

A sharp grunt interrupted her concentration. She
paused in her milking and looked toward the horses.

The workhorses were motionless. Likewise, Molly
was standing calmly, her nose to one corner, serenely
swishing her tail. Next to Molly, Jezebel held her head
at alert, gazing at her.

Odd. It must have been Jezebel, but something was
not quite right about that sound. There had been
something rather unhorselike about it.

Annabelle began again, and this time continued
without interruption. She removed a pail one-third
full of milk, untied Elizabeth, and put her back in her
stall. She went on to Mary, a very sedate old cow, and
led her out to the passage.

Something moaned.

Annabelle stopped in her tracks. Standing silently, gripping the cow's halter, she listened. Her heart pounded in her ears and beat painfully in her neck.

Something was in here.

She heard nothing . . . nothing . . . and nothing. She began to breathe again. She had been mistaken. . . .

No, she had not. The moan was soft this time . . . and it was above her. Her breath stilled, Annabelle raised her eyes to the loft.

There was nothing to see. Whatever was there was back out of sight. Good lord, what should she do? She should get Joseph . . . or Angus. But suppose they found nothing? She would appear silly, plus Lizzie's fears would be confirmed.

Fear running through her like a dose of salts, Annabelle released Mary and crept quietly to the loft ladder. Beside it was a hayfork, and she took it. For one moment she stood silently and stared at the ladder, dread, duty, and common sense locked in a hopeless mêlée. Then, with her hitched-up skirts secured by her apron and the hayfork clutched awkwardly in one hand, she climbed the ladder as silently as a whisper.

At the top, she raised her head very, very slowly and peered over the straw-strewn floor. It was dimly lit, save for the pale light coming from the small window cut at the gable.

At first she saw nothing. Silently, she advanced another rung, then another. At last, slowly and carefully, she set foot upon the loft floor and drew herself up. Standing tall, she took a last survey.

The pile of straw in the corner shifted. Before her shocked eyes it grew, forming a massive shaggy head and coarse wooly shoulders, quivering, shuddering, and lurching in an attempt to rise.

Heaven preserve me. The creature appeared to be a man—the most horrifying, wretched thing she had seen in her life!

She watched like a dumb thing until the man-creature found its feet. Her own were useless, and her limbs felt made of lead. As the ghastly man-creature straightened, she suddenly realized the wooly skin was a loose robe—just as the robe fell open, revealing all that a maiden of good standing should never view before her wedding night.

Shock—and proof that the creature was indeed very human—spurred her to action. She snatched up the hayfork and thrust it out in front of her, the sharp wooden tines directed straight at the man's midsection.

"Halt there! Come no closer, or I—or I will run you through!"

He made no advance, but stood there, swaying on his feet, staring at her dumbly. Then, he looked down and caught sight of himself. He hesitated, as if confused.

"I—I beg your—"

It was more a croak than a voice. Then, he fell face-first into the straw.

Chapter Two

"*Y*ou are never bringing that filthy beggar in here!" cried Mrs. Bottom. Mrs. Bottom stood in the front hall with an expression of dismay, staring at the alarming vision entering through the front doors of Hartleigh Hall.

"Indeed, I am," said Annabelle. "Joseph, I have decided upon Father's room. It is only one flight of stairs to carry him. Angus, take care with his head!"

"Your father's room!" Mrs. Bottom flung her floury hands outward. "The Lord help us!"

"I sincerely hope He does," Annabelle said. Preceding Joseph and Angus, who carried the unconscious man between them, she started up the stair. "The Lord surely knows we need it."

She credited Joseph with extreme restraint. She had even noticed his lips quiver once or twice and was certain she was about to hear his disapproval—but none came.

She opened her father's chamber, uninhabited since her sire's death, and went to fling open the curtains of the near window.

"Put him in the bed, please. Remove his—that thing he has on and burn it." She rounded the bed, crossing the path of Joseph and Angus, and flung open the curtains of the second window. She heard the men scuffling behind her with their limp burden, and catching a waft of her unwashed guest, she quickly threw open the casements.

"Please tell me when I may turn around," she said.

There was the sound of a soft impact and the rustle of the bed coverings being adjusted.

"You may turn, Miss Dearborn," said Joseph gravely.

She did, and viewed her two servants, both with their pained expressions poorly hidden. "You must wash him immediately," she said.

Joseph sighed audibly, a certain sign of his degree of concern. "Miss Dearborn, I must remind you of the possible danger this man represents—"

"He is no danger whatsoever. He is as helpless as a mouse."

"He will awaken."

"I heard him speak, Joseph. He was trying to pardon himself when he fainted. I have a feeling he is not the reprobate he looks."

"Nevertheless, there is doubt, and you have your guests and reputation to consider."

"He will harm no one. One of you will always keep watch. And as to his appearance . . ." She walked to her father's wardrobe and flung it open. From a shelf she drew out a clean linen shirt and held it open at arm's length.

"Father's clothes will do. Luckily he is a large man, for they are of a size. We shall tell the others he is a traveler in need of a good rest. That should allay any doubts."

She lowered the shirt and tossed it upon the near chair. She looked then once more at the men, who stood beside the bed of the stranger like reluctant mourners. The man, who lay on his back with the coverlet pulled to his unkempt chin, did indeed look quite deathlike.

"Joseph," she said quietly, and waited until she caught his eye. "I shall order a bath. You know what needs to be done. Angus, you must aid Joseph. And . . . I do sincerely thank you both for your help."

Leaving no time for further protest, she immediately quitted the room.

"Madame will see you."

Celeste, Madame's wizened little servant, creaked as she bowed, then turned and minced back into Madame's chamber, her ancient black bombazine leaving a musty trail in her wake. Annabelle took a deep breath, inhaling this scent and a strange perfume emanating from the room, both as mental fortification and to recover from the climb. Then she followed.

Madame's chamber was on the topmost floor of the house, but not because Madame la Comtesse was a charity resident, which she essentially was, along with her ancient Celeste. The room was, rather, where Madame preferred to be.

Fortunately Madame rarely wished to go out, for she could no longer manage the stairs. When she did, it required both Joseph and Angus to assist her, with Lizzie and Annabelle to the fore and Celeste to the rear. But Madame liked the pitched ceiling, which reminded her of the castle in which she once lived, she said—and she liked to gaze out across the countryside from her window, so she could have the advantage of warning should her "enemies" approach.

Annabelle stepped within and paused, and by habit

scanned the room for changes. Madame's main chamber was decorated with a number of archaic artifacts: a water-stained and brown-spotted rendering of the coat of arms of Louis XIV; a portrait of a young woman painted on wood and framed in gilt, which Madame had said was of herself; a large piece of Turkish tapestry, taking up all of one wall, the worse for the damage of mice; and an ancient brass and leather-bound trunk, which to Annabelle's knowledge, was never opened. There was no evidence of any addition or removal. The room looked, as always before, as if nothing whatsoever had been touched.

Madame herself sat in a regal chair, upholstered in faded red velvet, with an embroidered woolen robe over her lap. She wore the long-waisted, full-skirted robe in the style of the last century, her old body held firmly upright by a tightly laced bodice, her green striped white satin gone brown, and her white lace gone yellow. But the large gold chain and locket around her neck still glittered when she moved.

Madame was gazing out the window as she always did, her lean face and aristocratic nose in sharp profile, not looking at Annabelle at all.

Everyone else in the house thought the old woman was insane at worst or in her dotage at best. Annabelle's mother thought *Annabelle* was insane for allowing the old French expatriate to stay. Privately, Annabelle thought that her mother might have the right of it, but she could not bear to throw Madame and her faithful Celeste out. Clearly they were both helpless.

Comtesse or no, if Madame had experienced the guillotining of her family and by the grace of God had escaped, Annabelle would not be the one to destroy whatever fantasy she clung to. So Annabelle curtsied and waited for Madame to speak.

"They have not yet come," Madame said in her surprisingly deep voice. "The barbarous *cochons*."

"No, they have not," Annabelle said. "I believe you are quite safe."

"One is never safe from *them*," snapped Madame.

"To be sure."

Madame was silent a moment, then spoke again. "Of course, in my present situation of siege, I cannot yet provide for you. You must do what you can for now for *peu de temps*."

Annabelle held in the sigh, however much she had expected Madame's words. "Very well, Madame. I shall do my best."

"That is my brave one. It shall be but little more time, *j'espère*."

Madame said no more. Annabelle curtsied again and backed out the chamber door.

No payment from Madame again . . . not that she had expected it, only hoped. Annabelle descended the stairs, her mind racing to find yet another alternative to selling the ring. If she could strike upon some idea . . . but what? And for that matter, how much would the ring bring—and how long would it provide for them?

And now, she had yet another nonpaying guest, one who Joseph was convinced would murder them in their beds. Was she going daft, perhaps?

It had been more than an hour since she had left the destitute gentleman in Joseph's care, and she decided it was time to see what she could learn about him.

A half hour later she walked into her father's chamber bearing a bowl of soup prepared by a very ill-tempered Mrs. Bottom. Angus sat by the far side of the bed, looking uncomfortable in his domestic role. Joseph met her at the door and accompanied her to the bed, giving the impression that he would perish before he would leave her side.

Before her on the bed lay her guest, propped up on pillows, wearing her father's clean white shirt, with a swath of linen bandaged around his head. The whole of his face was bruised and scraped, but at least now it was clean of dirt and blood. He lay with his eyes closed, his breathing so light as to be hardly noticed.

She sat carefully in the chair by his near side, holding the bowl of soup. The fragrance drifted. His eyes, blackened and swollen, cracked open. From behind narrow slits, they moved to take in the bowl she held; and then, his gaze rose and focused on her.

For a moment he stared as though uncomprehending. Then he swallowed and made a weak attempt at clearing his throat. Still, his whisper was intelligible when he spoke.

"Who are you?" he asked.

The woman's face appeared to him in a haze, with only the shape of her shoulders and her scent verifying to him she was female. Mixed in with the light, sweet scent she wore was the aroma of food, which made his dry mouth water and his stomach tighten into an anxious knot. Damme, he hoped that soup—or whatever it was he smelled from the bowl she held—was for him. He was near wresting it from her he was so hungry, but he was as weak as a kitten—and, besides, that would be extremely bad behavior.

She spoke. "Who am I? That is an odd question. It was to be my question to you. After all, you are in my house."

"I am?"

The room was a blur. Moving his eyes slightly, he made out a dark shape beside her, a man, but he could not see enough to make out the room.

"I have not been here before, then?"

"No, you have not," she said. "Perhaps you might tell me who you are."

He swallowed again. The scent of food was making him dizzy. "I—" *Oh, bloody hell.* "I do not know."

"You do not know who you are?" She sounded skeptical, as well she might. "How did you come to be in my stable?"

So that was where he had been. Clearly, he had been in someone's stable, but his memory of that was now hazy as well.

"I . . . I walked . . . a long way."

"How did you come to be in the state you are in?" He heard her stir, the rustle of her gown.

"I—" Merciful heaven. She held a spoon poised before his mouth—close, but not close enough.

His throat felt full of sand. "I do not know. Truly. I do not." His voice cracked.

The spoon moved closer. Desperately he reached for it with his mouth, bumped it, and felt the soup run down his chin.

"You had best let me do it," came a man's voice.

"No, I can manage very well, thank you, Joseph."

The spoon appeared before him again. "Gently, sir. Open your mouth and let me do the rest."

This time he exercised all his self-control and let her.

"Very good. Now another."

Mercifully, she fed him for some minutes before she asked him another question.

"I have a mystery I should like solved," she said. "It

involves my cows and my hens. Have you perhaps availed yourself of them in the last few days?"

He tried to remember. What came to him was the terrible struggle to climb the ladder to the loft. It was a wonder he had accomplished it.

He took a fortifying breath and noted that his throat had been somewhat soothed. "I . . . may have done."

"You are not certain?" She was holding the spoon just out of reach again.

"I do not know." He paused, but the spoon came no closer. "I must have. I seem to be . . . all turned about."

She continued to feed him and did so until the bowl was empty.

"Perhaps later you will recall more," she said. "You are a little feverish at present, but some nourishment and care should help."

"I . . . am grateful."

"And I," she said, rising, "am too softhearted, as Joseph would say if he dared. But I am not foolish, and so you will not be left alone."

She started to step away, then paused. "I think someone is very concerned for you and looking for you at this moment."

He stared until she turned, then closed his eyes. Could that be true? He had no idea who he was. Perhaps he had no one. Perhaps he was a stray soldier, some poor wandering soul with no home. He certainly wished it were otherwise.

He sensed when she left, and the loneliness took him to sleep.

Annabelle spent the next three days fretting silently, in turns berating herself for taking in yet another non-paying guest, then taking herself to task for questioning the only decision an honorable person could have made. But her coffers were frighteningly low, Joseph had been unusually silent, Mrs. Bottom muttered and scolded Lizzie, Lizzie cried, and Angus grumbled. Annabelle feared that if Angus spent a few more days with the new guest and without liquid comfort, he would one morning be gone.

Only Mother had been her usual self, concerned with her daily comforts and cheerful when it suited her—which was more often than usual. However, Annabelle had told Mother nothing about the true circumstances of the new guest. Mother was planning the expenditure of the new guest's payments by considering new draperies in the drawing room.

Rather than face the object of her worries, Annabelle had not visited the guest again. For the past four days she had been busying herself, accompanying Lizzie during the milking; supervising the housemaids, Neda and Bab, in a thorough cleaning of the common rooms, sorting linen for mending; and tending the kitchen garden for Mrs. Bottom. This morning she gave herself a reprieve and set upon a solitary walk in the more extensive ornamental garden behind the manor, cutting blooms for the buffet and the drawing room.

It was cool, but Annabelle had a few beads of sweat on her brow as she paused in her task and gazed at the rambling rose which climbed the garden wall. There was a late bloom, high up, a difficult reach. In the overgrown garden, blooms were becoming hard to find. In the knotted-up pouch of her apron, she had fewer than she had set her heart upon.

Her pause was long enough for her to feel the prickle of worry she had been avoiding by her strenuous busy-ness. Shoving it back, she stepped up to the shrub and reached.

Her fingers came just short of the blossom, stretch as she would. Grasping the thorny bough to bring it closer was to invite bloody punctures and scratches from the thorns.

In that instant she felt a warm presence at her side. Before she could react, a man's arm reached past her and plucked the rose.

Annabelle whirled. Startlingly close to her stood a tall stranger, calmly offering her the purloined bloom.

Annabelle smothered a gasp, took a step back, and felt a tough cane of briars dig into her shoulder. She could do nothing then but stand and stare up at him.

His dark hair was tied in a simple queue. There was a gash at his temple, not quite healed, and a scrape on his cheekbone. If not for those and the bruising still apparent around his eyes, she would not have known him.

"I am sorry," he said. "I did not mean to startle you, Miss Dearborn." He held out the rose, waiting.

His voice was rather deep with a distinct huskiness that made a prickling run up her spine. It was also refined and polite, not the accent of any brigand she could imagine. In fact, it seemed the stranger was born of gentry.

She let out her breath and reached out for the blossom. Her fingertips just brushed his when she accepted it.

She gave him a more comprehensive look. His face was cleanly hewn with well-defined cheekbones. His mouth was firm, his eyes a deep mahogany brown. He wore her father's shirt; her father's fawn waistcoat; and her father's knee breeches, leggings, and boots. The breeches were too large at the waist, and it appeared he had pinned them.

Lastly, he carried her father's rosewood cane, and he leaned on it now.

She glanced discreetly past him and quickly around. There was not a soul in sight. She was alone in the garden with the stranger, and here by the garden wall she was certain they could not be seen from the manor.

She brought her gaze back to him. Even if he was born of gentry as his speech indicated, the circumstances of his discovery and claimed lack of memory made her anxious.

"I—I supposed Angus was with you." Inside her apron, she tightened her fingers around the handle of her small kitchen knife.

"He was. He is asleep in his chair. I saw no reason to disturb him." ·

The gentleman held her in a steady perusal, but it was not threatening. Rather, it was questioning.

"I feel quite well this morning," he said, "and I find I have regained some of my strength. I dislike confinement. Furthermore, I hoped to speak with you."

Annabelle's heart fluttered. The man's proximity was doing strange things to her equilibrium, and that brought a new rush of anxiety.

"Have you remembered your name?"

"I am afraid not." He paused. "You are in need of help."

Annabelle stared. "You are observant!" His abrupt change of subject surprised her.

"I should like to make a proposal." He paused again. "Miss Dearborn, I am clearly in a difficult spot. I do not know who I am or where I should go. I do believe I can be of assistance to you. I would like to work for my bed and board . . . for a short while, at least."

She stood silently, gazing at him, grappling with this new idea and finding her case of nerves made rational thought extremely difficult. Her heart kept up its annoying throbbing at the base of her jaw, and she was convinced he could see the pulsing in her neck.

"I am asking for much, I realize," the man continued. "But I am certain I can prove my worth. I will not accept charity. I mean to repay it."

Annabelle's mind raced. The man, whoever he was, was well-bred. Even Joseph had suggested another manservant, and one could not be had for a better price. But she had not the slightest knowledge of who—or what—he was. As far as *his* not remembering his identity, she could only take his word for it—and appearances could be deceiving. She only knew that he did not strike her as a scoundrel.

"I should like time to think about this," she said.

For a long moment he simply regarded her expressionlessly, and she began to feel nervous once more. Then he spoke.

"Very well. That is most reasonable." He nodded politely. "Good morning to you."

He turned and left her. She gazed after his limping form, noting that for all he had suffered, there was a strength and assurance about him.

As he disappeared behind the small grove of apple trees, she found she was clutching tightly the stem of the rose.

Chapter Three

*A*nnabelle stared dumbly at the rose while her wits did a merry dance in her head. Then she dropped the bloom into her apron, wrenched herself loose from the thorny branch clinging to her shoulder, and ran after the stranger.

She stopped just around the first bend in the path. Ahead she saw the stranger had paused and was now having speech with Mr. Goodfellow.

For a moment she was seized by panic. Mr. Goodfellow, a stout man with a balding pate and considerable impatience with any inconvenience, would promptly raise a hue and cry at any sign of trouble. The stranger's battered appearance was alarming enough, but how would he explain himself? In a moment, however, she realized that Mr. Goodfellow was speaking in his usual loud and rapid manner, his expression betraying interest.

"I myself have come here to study and write. I have almost completed the third volume of a detailed treatise on the modernization of the mail. The improvement of the roads . . ."

Annabelle gave a sigh of relief.

She did not hear the stranger's reply, but Mr.

Goodfellow's hearty, "Good day to you, then!" came to her clearly on the breeze.

Immediately she set out again at a faster pace to catch the stranger before he encountered anyone else. However, she saw that she was destined to meet Mr. Goodfellow on the path as he proceeded toward her on his solitary promenade. The stranger continued on his way to the house, and in some distress she saw that her chances of catching him before he caused some problem or other were slim indeed.

"Miss Dearborn!" Mr. Goodfellow raised his walking stick in greeting. He was fully dressed in coat, overcoat, and high-crowned beaver hat, and was already sweating from heat and exertion.

He stopped before her, and she had no choice but to pause as well. He took out his kerchief, wiped his face, and carefully tucked it back inside his coat. All the while Annabelle felt like squirming in impatience.

"A fine fellow, that Mr. Wakefield!" Mr. Goodfellow said at last. "I gather he has just come. Very nice manner about him. Shows proper interest in matters of importance. You should have more guests like him."

Distracted by a distant glimpse of the stranger descending the steps to the kitchen door, she faltered at an answer.

"Mr. Wake—? Oh, yes. He has only—he arrived—a short time ago."

"He was in a ghastly carriage accident, he says. Appears to me that he is a lucky man. Says he means to recover here."

"Yes. Yes, quite."

"Well, I shan't keep you, Miss Dearborn. I must have my walk. Keeps the mind sharp. Good day!"

As soon as Mr. Goodfellow ambled past her and around the bend, Annabelle picked up her heels.

"Mr. Wakefield" was he? And what else had he told Mr. Goodfellow?

She caught up with "Mr. Wakefield" in the kitchen. She paused in the doorway and saw that she was indeed too late.

The stranger stood across the worktable from Mrs. Bottom. Mrs. Bottom had stepped back a pace from the table, where the mass of dough she had been kneading lay; in one hand she clutched a sturdy rolling pin, and in her eyes was steely determination.

"I do beg your pardon," the stranger was saying. "I did not intend to intrude. I seem to have lost my way."

"That," snapped Mrs. Bottom, "is no news to me and hasn't been since Miss Dearborn discovered you in the stable, with a belly full of my eggs and milk!"

"I mean no trouble. If you would only assist—"

"Oh, you want assistance, do you?" Mrs. Bottom raised the rolling pin. "If you do not leave my kitchen *now*, you will *have* my assistance!"

At this point Annabelle felt it prudent to make her presence known.

"There you are!" Annabelle said loudly, stepping into the kitchen. "No need to bother yourself, Mrs. Bottom. I was about to show Mr. Wakefield to his room when I was waylaid by Mr. Goodfellow." She advanced on the stranger, giving him a speaking look. "Come with me, *Mr. Wakefield*."

He had the grace to look somewhat disconcerted.

"I am in your debt. Thank you."

He followed her meekly enough through the kitchen into the hall. She gave a silent prayer of thanks; she had no idea what he was thinking. He was either a great tease, or he was completely lacking in common sense.

Proceeding before him, her head held high in mock assurance, she said, "It surprises me that your memory has returned so suddenly. I am very eager to learn more about *Mr. Wakefield*."

He cleared his throat. "So am I. At the moment, all I know is that he *awakened* in a *field*."

She did not know whether to laugh or scold. Her heart throbbed annoyingly.

"Then you have remembered something!"

They turned to take the stair, and at that moment she glanced back at him and her gaze fastened on his face. His expression was sober and shielded. Even if he were not bruised, she felt she would not fathom the emotion behind his eyes.

"Well, um, yes," he said. "I remember waking in a ditch by the side of a road. I believe I must have been robbed. From there I made my way here. I am afraid, as information, it is little enough."

She looked ahead, placed her hand on the polished oak stair rail, and continued before him up the stairs.

"And you have introduced yourself to Mr. Goodfellow as Mr. Wakefield. Was that wise . . . Mr. Wakefield?"

"It seemed best that I supply a name. I should not like to alarm your guests."

"That is very thoughtful of you. I noticed you also supplied a story for yourself. I understand you are now a *guest*."

He cleared his throat. "I apprehend that this presents a problem. My sincere apologies. It was necessary that I think very quickly."

They reached the first floor and continued on to the next.

"One would expect to meet others when one leaves one's room and be prepared for the occasion.

In any case, you must be Mr. Wakefield now. But I have not made up my mind what to do about you yet. I cannot afford to trust on such little information. I am a charitable woman, Mr. Wakefield, but not a foolish one."

"I understand."

"It is a very good thing that you do."

They reached the second floor, where the main bedrooms were located, and Annabelle turned toward her father's room, her heart pounding more rapidly than was necessary from the climb. Mr. Wakefield followed one step behind.

"Am I to be imprisoned again?" he asked.

His words took her by surprise. Annabelle stopped short and turned to face him.

He stood gazing at her, a tall trim man in an ill-fitting suit of clothes, his face marred by scrapes and bruising, his eyes still surrounded by purplish rings. But the calm directness of his brown eyes commanded her respect . . . and something more. She did not recognize it, but she felt compelled to give a frank answer.

"I am not imprisoning you."

"You did make it clear that I was to be watched," he said. "That I understood. But now you are returning me to my room like a truant schoolboy."

She felt a moment's alarm until she spotted the trace of amusement in his eyes. Still, she had the oddest feeling that she was being examined, assessed . . . tested.

"You should wish to rest and regain your strength."

"I have had quite enough of that for the past four days. I shall return to my room to please you, but be warned: I am quite able to leave it again. Your Angus sleeps much better than he watches."

Annabelle held his eyes. There was a quality of self-possession in them that seemed to issue a subtle challenge.

A fluttering within her seemed to shake her reason. What was it? But no, it was not fear even now. It was something that tried to reach past her womanly guard, to rob her of control. She pressed it back, shutting it firmly behind the door that guarded all emotion. She could have none of that ever again.

She steeled herself. "What you mean, Mr. Wakefield, is that I should not delude myself that we are protected from you."

He bowed. "That is the matter precisely, Miss Dearborn. I quite appreciate your candor." His penetrating dark eyes locked with hers. "But I beg you to take this interpretation to its natural conclusion. It also means that I shall do you no harm. I have had the opportunity, but no inclination to do so."

Annabelle blinked. She disliked being defeated by reason; she herself was generally the one who ruled with logic. But her strange gentleman was besting her. Her odd emotional reaction to him had to be of her own doing, not his; he had actually said and done nothing to cause it.

"What are you asking of me?"

"Simply this—that you treat me as any other in your household. In exchange, while I remain here, I shall endeavor to make myself useful. I shall grant that I have made a very poor impression, arriving as I did; but I can only attempt to make up for it. That is, of course, if you allow me to do so."

Annabelle gazed at him, wondering what it was about this man that instilled trust, for that was what he was doing to her, as assuredly as she drew breath. She wondered if he knew something about himself that he had not told her, even so, for he did not seem so very concerned whether he remembered or not. And yet he gave no cause for alarm.

Then Annabelle thought of all the things an able man could do for her that faithful Joseph, and the errant Angus, could not.

She could not know what her Mr. Wakefield's walk of life had been—whether nobility, lesser gentry, or some bankrupt gentleman or cardsharp whose dealings had caught up with him—but he hardly seemed dangerous. And once he regained his full health and strength, which would seem to be very soon, there were many things she could set him to doing. She had food, thank the Lord, having a productive garden, the cows, the fowl, and the sheep. If he only desired meals and a roof for his services, she had the best possible solution to at least *some* of her problems.

She took a breath. "Mr. Wakefield," she said, "I have decided that you may stay and work for me. I suppose we must say you are doing so for your health, since you have told Mr. Goodfellow you are a guest, but you *shall* work."

"Oh, but absolutely, Miss Dearborn." Wakefield bowed again. "Would you wish me to do something now?"

"Oh . . . oh, no. I believe you should see to your health for another day or so. We shall speak again."

With that she turned and left him, rapidly descending the stairs and arriving quite breathless at the bottom. She placed a hand to her bosom and stared at the heavy oak front door of Hartleigh Hall, wondering if she were the sensible woman she had always thought herself to be.

* * *

Mr. Wakefield made his way to his room and then crossed to the looking glass that hung above the washstand. Staring at his strangely ravaged face, he touched a battered cheekbone tentatively with his fingertips and traced its shape slowly to his chin, where he paused.

It was a face he knew. Of course he did—it was his own. And yet it was so different. The terrible effects of the assault left the reflection of a creature that cast him into an agony of doubt.

This did not feel natural. He did not believe he customarily appeared to be such a loutish-looking fellow. Or could he be such an unsavory article? He remembered wondering if he had tipped the cups too much and had thus engaged himself in difficulties. Now he wondered again if that were indeed true.

His hand—it was scraped as well, and although he had thoroughly attended his toilette and cleaned and smoothed the ragged edges of his nails, it still bore the look of one who engaged in a more vulgar way of life. As he gazed at its reflection in the mirror, the hand began to shake.

He turned away from the mirror to discover his legs were trembling as well. He made his way to the bed, shakily climbed the steps, and lay flat out on the coverlet.

His heart pounded. His breath came shallowly, as if iron bands were about his chest. *Lord Almighty, I am in a most bedamned mess.*

Wakefield closed his eyes. This was what damnation felt like. *I do not know who I am, and I am afraid.* That was the simple truth. To work and work one's brain, and to have nothing from it: It was a torment beyond any he could imagine. Worst of all was a feeling that he *must* remember, that there was something very important he *must* do.

What cursed thing had happened to him?

Wakefield. How utterly clever of me. He released a sound of derision and placed a hand across his eyes. His forehead was slick with perspiration.

At least he had remembered awaking beside the road. If he'd been left with one stitch of his own, he might have some clue as to his identity, but he had been robbed of that as well. He was as a newborn babe, come into the world with a bare bottom and a mind as unadorned. What could he do? How could he open the gate to his memory?

What can I do, indeed? He gave in to this line of thought and made a mental list.

He could think. He knew the mother tongue. He felt he was an Englishman. He could . . . could do what? He raised his hand and looked up at it. Were these hands useful for anything? Did they know a trade? Or was he something quite different?

He gave up to despair and exhaustion. He had to rest; he had to regain his composure. He must not unduly concern Miss Dearborn. These things he knew.

The veils drew over him one by one, pulling him down farther and farther into sleep. It was then that he saw the face of the old man.

The visage was a severe one, with bushy white brows drawn close, the flesh above his aristocratic nose furrowed, his jaws clenched tight. The old eyes glittered like daggers' points. He raised a knobby finger and pointed it accusingly.

Then, his lips moved.

Wakefield strained with all the strength in his being . . . but he heard nothing. Nothing.

The last veil fell, and he was asleep.

* * *

Annabelle took a steadying breath and sought her inner strength, willing the heartbeat beneath her hand to slow. The stranger must not affect her. No man must affect her. She had to think of her home, Hartleigh, of her mother, and of herself. There was too much at stake.

In a moment she straightened her shoulders and was about to proceed when she heard a measured footfall behind her. She turned.

Joseph stopped and bowed. "Miss Dearborn, might I please have a word with you?"

Annabelle's chest tightened, defying her best effort at calm. "Of course, Joseph."

He followed her to the library, then stepped forward and opened the heavy door for her. She went inside and crossed to the armchair by the fireplace, and when she was seated, she nodded, and Joseph came to stand before her.

"Miss Dearborn, forgive me for what I am about to say, but I must speak or be very remiss in my duty. I am concerned about this man who has been allowed into your home."

Annabelle took a fortifying breath. "I guessed as much. I truly understand, Joseph, and I thank you for your observation."

"Miss Dearborn, I think that perhaps you do not understand the gravity of the situation. The potential for harm is certain. We know nothing of him but that he was decently breeched and that he has command of the King's English. He is now, I understand, wandering about unguarded and has given Mrs. Bottom a considerable turn. We must weigh this matter."

Annabelle withheld a sigh. She could not fault Joseph. He had long been more than a servant to her.

She depended upon him, perhaps, more than he knew.

"I am very mindful of the risk," she said, "but I feel Mr. Wakefield is quite harmless. I do think he can even be useful. He has agreed to work for me in return for bed and board, and in that sense he is truly a gift. You have said we need another manservant. Why not Mr. Wakefield?"

Joseph's eyebrows had assumed the winged look of incredulity. "Mr. Wakefield?"

"Oh, yes. That is how he is now styling himself. He recalls awakening at the side of the road, near a field, he says. In any case, he met Mr. Goodfellow on his walk this morning and was forced to think of some explanation for himself rather quickly. Thus he is now Mr. Wakefield, our guest, recovering from a carriage accident. But he will work for me all the same. He must say he wants to be busy, I suppose. I shall think of something."

Joseph's silence confirmed Annabelle's fears. Joseph was not won over.

"If Mr. Wakefield can be trusted," she said, "would this not be a good plan?"

Joseph took a deep breath. "If he can be trusted. And if our larder and garden hold out. We were unlucky with lambs this spring, as you know, and there is the bay with the lame leg. Jezebel has been borrowed for the plow, but she is very difficult. I understand the planting has not been going well. But of course, he must have the ability to be useful."

"Any man we hire must eat. And he will be useful if he needs to be."

Joseph sighed. "Very well, Miss Dearborn. I shall set myself to finding occupation for him, then. He might help Angus with the grounds, to start."

"Very good. But I do not think he should do heavy work just yet, and I should like to use him in the house first. Neda and Bab do not keep up. The dust is quite beyond anything."

Annabelle ended her interview with Joseph with a lighter heart. Matters would go better now; she knew they would. She must attend a few little things first, though: determine an explanation for Mr. Wakefield's service, for one, and for another convince Lizzie to milk once more without revealing that the egg and milk thief had been Mr. Wakefield. But all in all, matters boded well.

Annabelle's morning passed swiftly with the duties she was obliged to perform. Since losing the housekeeper, Annabelle had helped Mrs. Bottom supervise the housemaids, Neda and Bab, who today carried water up the stairs and the slops down; served the breakfast trays; cleaned the rooms; and gathered up soiled linens. She also saw Mrs. Bottom about the day's meals, compiled a list of needed supplies, and spoke to Joseph about any of his concerns regarding the buildings, the grounds, the fields, and the cattle.

It was time for tea before she anticipated it. Tea was served in the dining room for the Captain and Mr. Goodfellow, and a tray was sent up to Madame. Annabelle usually took her own tea alone or with her mother, but as Mother had been irritable earlier and complained of the headache, Annabelle anticipated a respite. She therefore carried her tea into the library, settled in a wing chair, then leaned back and closed her eyes, the tea forgotten beside her.

A scratching came at the library door. She opened her eyes.

"Come in."

Mrs. Thistle, her mother's lady's maid, opened the door. Tall and lean with an expression of aristocratic supremacy on her narrow face, Mrs. Thistle was generally liked by no one but Mother.

"Mrs. Dearborn desires her tea and would see you in her chambers," she said.

Annabelle felt a very undaughterly regret. "Very well. Tell Mother I shall be there shortly."

Mrs. Thistle raised her chin. "I am bringing up the tea directly, and my mistress reads at half past the hour. She shall need you before then."

"Give my message to Mother, please. You may go."

Annabelle sensed Mrs. Thistle's offended sensibilities as Thistle closed the door behind her. Annabelle considered that the irritating woman should be glad of her employment.

"'My mistress reads at half past the hour'!" Annabelle sputtered. She picked up her tea and poured, determined to have a few sips before going upstairs. It was only a short while later that she arose and proceeded to her mother's room.

Visits with her mother could be unpleasant, not because her mother was an unpleasant person, but because Mrs. Dearborn clung to the pretense of station by her neatly shaped and buffed fingernails. To Mother, economizing was a ghastly thing done by someone else. She knew that Father had lost their money; she knew that Annabelle had lowered herself to take in lodgers. But to Mrs. Dearborn, none of that had any effect upon her. It was, Annabelle felt, a kind of blindness. And so Mother kept her Mrs. Thistle, and only the remainder of the household felt any pinch.

Annabelle arrived at her mother's door and entered

the chamber to find her mother on her chaise, enfolded in her dressing robe, sipping her tea.

"There you are, Annabelle. Thistle, you may go and freshen my gown now. The taffeta, I think. No, the bombazine."

"The crepe would suit the weather today," said Thistle.

"That is too light. I cannot afford to take cold."

"You may have your woolen wrap with it."

Annabelle sat in the wing chair by the fireplace and waited in silence while Mother chose which black afternoon gown to wear. Annabelle began going over expenses in her head and was thus surprised when Mother's raised voice came through her reverie.

"Annabelle, have you heard what I have said?"

Annabelle jolted. "Yes, Mother." She glanced up and saw her mother's wry look.

Mrs. Dearborn's arched brows rose even higher. "Do not attempt to fool me, young lady. You have not listened at all."

"I am sorry, Mother. I have things on my mind."

"Nothing all that important, I hope?"

"Nothing that cannot wait."

"Good. For I have an idea for changing around the drawing room and wished to discuss it with you. The draperies are a disgrace, and the upholstery is positively a horror. We cannot have proper guests in to sit upon threadbare cushions! I have decided upon colors and shall begin working the seat covers straight away, but we simply *must* have new draperies. I am determined upon gold damask. I have given it thought, and there is nothing for it but that we must make a journey to London."

"Mother—"

"Do not make excuses. We shall stay with your aunt Holden. Joseph may attend to matters here. I am certain you can be spared."

Mrs. Thistle was at Mother's dressing table, arranging this and that, presumably putting things in order. Annabelle took a settling breath. "We need privacy, Mother."

Her mother frowned. "Whatever for? We may speak before Thistle."

Annabelle pressed her lips together, giving her mother a speaking look.

Mother gestured impatiently. "Oh, very well. Thistle, you may go."

Thistle left. Annabelle waited a safe interval, knowing that Thistle was happiest listening at the door.

"Mother, we cannot afford new draperies, and I cannot go to London."

Mother sat rigidly upright. "Cannot afford draperies? How shall we keep up appearances? Your father would not have allowed such a thing!"

This was a painful blow—the cost of doing battle with her mother. Annabelle stiffened her spine. "We have no company to speak of, and so it is of no consequence. We shall not use the drawing room for visitors, that is all."

"And no wonder we have no company. You have lowered yourself to a common drudge! Not going to London! I suppose you do not want to run the risk of meeting an eligible gentleman."

"As you know, Mother, our circumstances make it impossible for any eligible gentleman to be interested."

Mother leaned back on the chaise once more, her attitude resentful and angry. She picked up her handkerchief and kneaded it in her hands.

"You might have married Mr. Harwell."

"We lost our money, Mother. There was no help for it."

"You released him!"

"Because it would have been a worse scandal had he been forced to cry off."

Mother carefully straightened out her handkerchief and folded it with unconscious precision. "And the amount that was spent on your come-out clothes. All of those gowns, gone to waste!"

Annabelle said nothing.

"You are past wearing the white muslins. I may as well pluck off all that expensive ribbon and lace and use the material for something. Heaven knows we will have no new caps else!"

Again Annabelle did not answer.

Mother tucked the handkerchief in her bodice. Her embroidery was beside her on the chaise; she picked it up.

"I supposed that new . . . *guest* is paying us for his stay. What of that? It must afford us something."

Mother worked determinedly on the embroidery, not looking up from it. Annabelle closed her eyes for a moment and sighed silently.

"He is truly a guest, Mother. Knowing our circumstances, he has agreed to do some tedious things for me. We dreadfully need the assistance."

Mother paused in her embroidery and looked up. Her gray eyes pierced like shards of ice. "What? He does not *pay*? And I may not purchase new draperies? Has your mind gone completely begging?"

Annabelle swallowed. Doubt and guilt crept past her guard, and a quiver of unease ran up her spine. Had this man duped her? Perhaps she was not made of the stuff needed to save their home. Slowly, day by day, their meager finances worsened. Her plan *must* work, however. It must, or there was but one alternative for her.

"The work needs to be done, Mother, and there is no one else to do it. He can help put the grounds to order. Make repairs. Any number of things."

"Can he repair the roof?"

As she sometimes did, Mother surprised by revealing an astute understanding beneath her veil of denial.

"Yes." Annabelle had no idea if the stranger knew how to repair a roof. It was a fair guess that he did not.

"That is all very well, Annabelle, but a roof that does not leak will not keep you from a fate as governess for some encroaching cit, should it come to that. And as I see matters, it will. I can hardly support you. I suppose I shall have to retire to some beastly small house in Bath, with no room but for myself and Thistle."

Mother's tongue had thrown another lethal dart and spoke to the fate Annabelle most feared. Annabelle sat rigidly, clutching her cold hands together, praying they were hidden in the folds of her dress.

Annabelle knew that the fate that loomed was worse than Mother could conceive. Mother could not afford that beastly small house in Bath; and in such dire circumstances, Thistle would not be induced to stay. Mother's portion had been devastated, also.

There simply must be *some* way to recover.

"Harwell," Mother said, "would have had a man repair the roof, and the matter would have been done with. And he would have purchased the draperies with no objection whatsoever."

Annabelle left the room before her pain escaped in words she would regret. Blinded by her bitter hurt, she strode into the hall—straight into a tall, unyielding obstacle. She recoiled, and two strong hands clasped her upper arms.

"I beg your pardon," he said.

Annabelle looked up to meet the dark eyes of her stranger in residence, Mr. Wakefield.

Chapter Four

*H*e awoke in a panic. He found himself sitting bolt upright on the side of the bed, gasping for breath, with no idea whatsoever why. Still, something yet teased at the edge of his memory, dancing in and out, and with mighty effort he seized at it—and failed. It was gone.

Wakefield. That was who he was. John Wakefield, named by himself and known by no one, birthed in a ditch here in . . . Leicestershire. Damn, that was it. He needed a map.

He leapt out of bed, paused for a moment at the looking glass to compose himself, and then stepped out into the hall.

He heard the faint sounds of voices immediately. They were indistinguishable, but female. Glancing up the hall, he encountered the startling vision of a thin woman bent over at the next door, listening intently, her pointed derriere protruding in his direction. His reaction was instant.

"Madame, recall yourself."

The woman straightened sharply and faced him. She looked startled and mortified. "Sir!"

He walked toward her, frowning. "Go about your business. *Now*, if you please."

The woman stared at him, as though at a loss. Then she abruptly turned and walked up the hall, her back ramrod straight.

He paused and watched her departure, and wondered at himself. His reaction had been natural, and yet he was not in the position to take a superior tone. It meant something. But the voices intruded on his thoughts.

". . . will not keep you from a fate as governess for some encroaching cit, should it come to that. And as I see matters, it will. I can hardly support you. I suppose I shall have to retire to some beastly small house in Bath, with no room but for myself and Thistle."

He noted that the door had been left ajar, and he was now standing right before it. He realized he should walk on, but now he was as fixed as the unscrupulous servant had been.

There was no reply from the other woman in the room. The first spoke again. "Harwell would have had a man repair the roof, and the matter would have been done with. And he would have purchased the draperies with no objection whatsoever."

There was the sound of rustling . . . a light step. Before he could move, the door was flung open—and a woman walked smack into him.

Instinctively he clasped her upper arms, steadying her. "I beg your pardon," he said.

Annabelle. She looked up to meet his eyes. Hers were the loveliest shade of cognac, very wide and very startled.

She took in her breath sharply. "You!"

She stood staring at him and said nothing more. She seemed struck dumb.

He felt as dismayed as she appeared to be. The occasion called for the use of his tongue, however.

"I confess I cannot rest. I have only just risen."

She opened her mouth, closed it, and opened it again. "You were listening at the door!"

"Never. I did hear your voice. I wanted to speak with you. This seems, however, to be an inopportune time."

"I find that—that very unlikely, Mr. Wakefield!" She shrunk back from him and gave a little pull, and he realized he still held her arms. He released her.

"Again, I apologize."

Her scent came to him, the faint sweet scent of soap and roses. Fingers of afternoon light filtered in through the tall hall window and touched her light brown hair, rendering the stray strands a glittering gold.

As if she understood his thoughts, she reached up and deftly smoothed her hair, checking that it was still held tightly in place at the back of her head.

She was so slender. A good wind would take her. And her face—such a pretty heart-shaped face, with a lovely little nose and soft, rosy lips.

"You need not stare."

He was, of course, doing just that.

"I do not mean to. I am sorry to have upset you."

"You have not upset me. It takes much more than a—a bumping to upset me."

"I see. Well, then, perhaps you might tell me where I may find a map?"

She looked at him as if he had gone mad.

"A map? So you can see how far you are from the home you cannot recall?"

"No, so I can read the names of towns and places. I might remember something."

"If that is all, you may follow me to the library."

She turned abruptly, as much to hide her distress as go about her business, he thought; and they had soon descended one floor and entered the library.

It was a large room considering the size of the manor, which although comfortable was not of kingly dimensions. There was a divan in the center of the room facing the fireplace, with a largish occasional table behind it, one with delicately curved legs and inlaid with rosewood, a single silver candelabra upon it. The carpet appeared to be Turkish, very old and quite worn. The odd armchair resided here and there, and the wall shelves held a respectable number of books. But on the whole, the room had the air of sad neglect.

He walked to the nearest shelf and withdrew a volume. The faded gilt lettering proclaimed it to be a tome on the history of the Ottoman Empire. He opened it.

"If it is a map of England you wish to see, it is here," she said.

He looked up to see her open a large volume on the table. He snapped his closed, and the dust exploded from the book.

"That was unwise," came her voice.

He could not see her because he was sneezing.

He heard her laugh. In the next moment she was pressing a handkerchief into his hand, and he speedily wiped his nose.

"I see I shall have to provide you with another dust cloth," she said cheerfully. "I shall bring you one. I think you have a good afternoon's work before you."

"A dust cloth?"

"Yes, that is what I said. The whole of this room needs a good cleaning. It is too little used, and the books are full of dust. I have just discovered a job for you, Mr. Wakefield."

She went cheerfully on her way to find him the cloth; and he looked after her, a softness forming in his breast where once there had been only fear. She was a lovely thing—not by the common standard, perhaps, but lovely just the same. It was not her face alone, not her shining burnished-oak hair, not her slender form—but her courage, and her heart.

He wondered who Harwell was. It was a fruitless curiosity, when he did not even know himself; but it was then he resolved to know, regardless of reason.

Annabelle escaped the library and walked purposefully up the hall. Pausing for but an instant, she glanced about herself and, seeing no one, ducked into the first room where she knew she would be private—her father's study. Closing the door behind her, she leaned up against its cool surface and closed her eyes.

You might have married Mr. Harwell.

As usual, Mother had used words like arrows, sharp and accurate, and certain arrows were difficult to forgive.

It was not my fault. But then why was she fighting tears?

She still remembered how the invitations had stopped coming. She remembered waiting those days for her fiancé to call—how, when he did come, he had been cool and distant, and rose to leave far too soon. Then she had looked into his face and saw that his eyes had changed.

A warm trickle started down her cheek and she dashed it away.

Mother seemed determined to blame her for all. It was true that advice had come to Annabelle by way of her aunt's friend Lady Locksley and not from Mother. But what else could have been done? Lady Locksley's words were nearly as painful today as when they had been said to her, and yet there had been no choice but to heed them. *You are no longer an eligible match for your fiancé. Do not force him to cry off. It would be very much better if you do so yourself. It is scandal enough without the gentleman taking measures.*

Mother, however, only saw crushed dreams.

They had removed from London shortly thereafter. The following winter, Annabelle's father had become ill.

Annabelle found herself staring at his work desk. The cobwebs before her eyes lifted, and she saw it as it appeared now, too neat, too vacant.

It seemed that the men in her life had a horrible habit of leaving. How odd that she must carry the burden of punishment for it.

Annabelle drew a deep breath, drawing strength from deep within. That had been quite enough of feeling sorry for herself. Now she had to go on. Mr. Wakefield would be wondering what happened to her. Mr. Wakefield . . .

It was perhaps due to her recent emotional state, but she was caught with a surprising feeling for Mr. Wakefield. She quite liked him. Around him she felt . . . safe.

Absurd! Oh, foolish! Had her remaining wits become addled? A nameless man without a pocket for a shilling! A man who might be, for all she knew, a clever sort of scoundrel! And here she was a woman who had learned her lesson quite well about the danger of blind trust, and certainly of attachments.

She turned abruptly and left the study, closing the door firmly behind her, and headed for the servants' stairs en route to the housekeeper's closet. She had the misfortune, however, to meet Mrs. Thistle coming up.

"There you are, Miss Dearborn!" she exclaimed.

Annabelle paused at the top of the stairs, awaiting Mrs. Thistle's ascent, noting the woman was a good deal more agitated than usual.

Mrs. Thistle took a great breath. "I must speak to you immediately!"

"You may speak to me here, if you wish." Annabelle had no desire to closet herself with Thistle, certainly not an agitated Thistle.

Thistle stopped before her at the top of the stair, a little breathless, her usually pallid cheeks a surprising shade of pink.

"That—that *man* you have taken in—I must say, he has addressed me in a most improper way! I cannot abide it! And he not even a guest, no matter what is said, for I know the truth! I have spoken to Bottom and Angus, and they have both confirmed it."

"Mrs. Thistle, whatever are you talking about? What has he done?" Annabelle's blood ran cold. *Was Wakefield a seducer of servants?*

"I shall tell you! He is nothing more than a—a—I do not know what, but I know that he was found in the stable wearing nothing but—"

"Thistle, *please!*" Annabelle shot a hurried glance around them and returned an admonishing look to Thistle.

Thistle paused. For an instant she recovered her

breath and at the same time appeared to regain some of her usual composure.

"What did he do?" Annabelle asked quietly.

"He spoke to me in a way I simply will not tolerate."

"How was that?"

"As if he were my—my *superior*. It is monstrous."

A wave of relief flooded Annabelle—and wickedly, a bit of delight. "I see. And what was it that he said?"

Thistle seemed to be considering her complaint carefully now. Annabelle found it worthy of note.

"He told me to—to go about my business, as though he had any right to. I *was* about my business, of course! He knows nothing about my business!"

"I see. What business were you about?"

Thistle's eyes snapped, but nothing else betrayed her. "Something quite ordinary, I assure you. I was carrying one of your mother's gowns in the hall. I had . . . paused. I had thought I had dropped a paper of pins."

"How strange. Have you told Mother?"

Thistle raised her chin. "Of course not. Your mother is in another of her states. She will be down with the headache for the day. I should not bother her with such a thing as this."

Annabelle knew that she, the errant daughter, was the reason for her mother's state and did not in the least wish to discuss this with Thistle.

"Then thank you for coming to me, Thistle."

Thistle nodded. "Very good, Miss."

"And I might caution you to say *nothing* of what you believe of Mr. Wakefield to anyone. We cannot afford to disturb the guests. I shall speak to him."

Thistle did not look entirely satisfied, but as she also appeared to wish the conversation ended, the conclusion was agreeable to both. As soon as Thistle's back was turned, Annabelle smiled and descended the stairs quite pleased over the encounter.

She had one more reason to like Mr. Wakefield, and this reason she could find no fault with whatsoever.

Two full hours passed before Annabelle was able to return to check on Wakefield's cleaning progress in the library. She found herself somewhat anxious as she arrived at the library door, but was completely surprised at what she found.

Wakefield stood in the center of the room at the inlaid rosewood table. He was deeply absorbed by an open volume, a thin line of concentration marking his high forehead. Around him on the table were assorted stacks of books—some open, some closed, stacked willy-nilly in piles of varying heights, some in danger of sliding to the floor. Some of the books, in fact, were actually upon the floor, piled thoughtlessly within a semicircle about his feet.

Mr. Wakefield was covered with a powdery film of dust . . . and so was everything else.

"*What* in heaven's name are you doing?"

Wakefield looked up, startled. There was a smudge of dust on the end of his regal nose and another on his chin, and his dark eyes were wide and bemused.

"I—er—good day, Miss Dearborn."

"'Good day!' Is that all you can say?" She stepped into the library and stood with arms akimbo, giving him an incisive look. "I asked you to clean, not—not to demolish!"

"I—" He paused, looked down at the table, then glanced about himself. "I . . . seem to have become distracted. I do beg your pardon." He looked back at her, his expression rueful. "You see, I found too much of interest . . ."

"Such as?"

She was enjoying herself. There was no doubt about it. There was a certain thrill in making a strong, imposing man come to his knees before her, so to speak. It made her wonder if she might be dangerous as the queen.

"Well . . ." He looked back at the open book before him. "I found I have previously read the history of ancient Greece, for instance. I seem to have knowledge of Latin. I comprehend that I am very knowledgeable of the globe. And I . . . I have an interest in Norman architecture."

"Norman architecture?"

He paused. "Yes."

"I see. And how is this useful?"

"Ah . . ." He paused again. "I do not know. I should not have mentioned it. Clearly it is not of particular relevance."

Annabelle cocked her head at him and studied his remorseful profile. She fought the smile that quirked at the corners of her lips.

"I should not say that any of that is of particular relevance to the task at hand. It is worse in this room than when you started."

He slowly turned his face to her. "I am sincerely sorry, Miss Dearborn."

"Do you believe you can make some improvement upon this mess?"

He blinked at her and then looked at the table. In a moment he found the cleaning rag lying beneath a discarded book. He picked up the rag and book, and then began whisking the cloth ineffectually at the book's cover.

"I should guess that dusting is not something you have learned to do." Annabelle walked up to him and plucked the rag and book from his hands.

"Apparently not." He paused for a moment. "Thank the graces."

She stared at him, not knowing how to accept his comment—then she noticed a flicker in his eyes that was not contrition.

Annabelle laughed.

"Clever wretch!" she said. "But not so clever as you may think, for I am going to *show* you how to dust these books." With a flourish she tucked the cloth in the pocket of her pinafore, held out the open book and began to clap its covers together.

"Egad!" Wakefield cried. He retreated several paces from her.

Annabelle stopped fanning the book, ran the cloth efficiently over its closed cover, spine, and edges, then held it up to him.

"*That* is how one dusts a book."

Wakefield took a deep breath and paused, screwed his face up terribly, then exploded in an enormous sneeze.

Annabelle put the book back upon the table. "Oh, dear."

He sneezed again.

"How is it that you can *read* them, but not *dust* them?"

Wakefield gave a half shake of his head and sneezed. Annabelle sighed, took out her handkerchief and handed it to him.

"No, I—I think I am finished," he said. He sniffed and gazed at her with watery eyes. "I have not done very well today, have I?"

Annabelle hesitated. It occurred to her that he had

indeed done her a service. "Actually, there is something else I need to speak to you about. Thistle seems to have taken a dislike to you."

"Thistle?"

"The servant you somehow offended by instructing her to go about her business."

His eyes flashed with comprehension. "Is she someone of importance?"

"She is my mother's personal maid."

He paused for a brief moment, and by his expression Annabelle realized he was framing something of significance to say to her.

"I dislike to reveal information of an unpleasant nature, but in this case, it is my duty to inform you . . . that Thistle listens at doors."

He looked concerned. He truly did. Annabelle could no longer help herself; something about this man was quite endearing.

"Is that all?" she asked. "I know all about Thistle's nose for news."

He frowned. "And you tolerate this?"

"No, but Mother does, so I must. Mother will hear nothing ill of Thistle."

"I must apologize. I had no business saying anything to her."

Annabelle studied his face. The swelling had gone down around his eyes, and the bruising was fading to pale green and yellow. His face was assuming its natural shape, and she realized that he might be very good-looking. But it was the expression of sincerity in his eyes that affected her the most.

She swallowed. "It would be best if you say nothing more to her. Thistle can cause trouble for you, and myself as well. Still, I must thank you. It is no small thing putting Thistle in her place."

His eyes softened, and she believed she perceived understanding in his careful expression. She was suddenly caught on a horrid precipice between guarding her privacy at all costs and falling into sympathetic arms and weeping her heart out. She could *not* be a fool.

Instead, she stepped toward him, plucked her handkerchief from his fingers, reached up, and began delicately wiping the smudge from his chin.

"Have you then seen anything in those books that brings your abilities to mind?" she asked. It was meant as a distraction, perhaps more for herself than for Mr. Wakefield.

He hesitated for a heartbeat and then spoke. "Nothing other than what I mentioned."

She reached higher and dabbed at the end of his nose. "You are an educated gentleman. Perhaps you do the Church's work. You have the right manner."

He captured her hand in his and gently conveyed it away from his nose.

"I think not," he said.

His deep brown eyes held her gaze, seeming to see too much. Annabelle felt her face bloom warm the very same way his hand was warming hers. She pulled her hand away from his gentle grasp.

"How can you know that?"

"I know because I do. 'How' I cannot tell you."

Her face felt no cooler, and her embarrassment grew. She frowned and stepped back from him.

"How can you know some things and not others?"

"I do not know."

She steeled herself to calm her quaking heart. Somehow he seemed to have got the upper hand, and she was in no mind to let it continue.

"I have formed the opinion," she said, "that I trust

what you show me much more than I trust your word. I think that from now on, I shall require you to demonstrate all to me, and *then* I shall be able to determine what you are capable of." She turned and started for the door. "Follow me."

"You wish me to say a sermon?" he asked.

"No. I wish you to milk a cow."

Chapter Five

Wakefield knew that Miss Dearborn was upset with him. Something had happened between them in the library, and he guessed what it was. Miss Dearborn was, as incredible as it seemed, battling an attraction to him.

He doubted very much she would even admit it to herself. Knowing how he appeared in the looking glass, he could appreciate why! But nevertheless she had become embarrassed and flustered, and now she was punishing him for it. So be it; if the punishment was for him to milk a cow, he would milk a cow.

He followed Miss Dearborn and her man Joseph to the stable, considering all that had happened between himself and Miss Dearborn, with an occasional thought to the cow. He had no idea if he could milk a cow, but he did have a healthy suspicion that he *should not* milk one.

His fate was sealed, however. Annabelle had ascertained that Angus had brought the cows in from pasture for the evening, and he was being led to his fate like a French aristocrat on a tumbrel. He carried the milk pail while Joseph walked ahead of him, between him and Miss Dearborn, and Wakefield was again reminded that the elderly retainer acted the guardian with his mistress. The fellow was not needed, but on learning Miss Dearborn was intent on a display of milking knowledge that very moment, Joseph had included himself on the trek to the stable.

As for Miss Dearborn . . . she had not looked at him since she had commanded that he follow her from the library. His only view of her during the descent downstairs, her conversation with Joseph, and their departure to the stable had been of the back of her pale blue figured gown. He had become sufficiently intimate with the back of this gown to detect a repair in the skirt, although small and expertly done.

He had also admired the graceful slope of her shoulders and delicate neck—and this in spite of the guilt he felt for holding her hand much too long in the library when he had only meant to remove her touch, and her temptation, from his face. He felt uncomfortably mortified with himself.

Joseph opened the stable door and allowed both Miss Dearborn and Wakefield to enter, and Wakefield felt Joseph's watchful eyes on the back of his neck. Miss Dearborn stepped in front of a stall and turned, finally, to face him.

"Here is Elizabeth," she said. "She is used to gentle hands."

"Elizabeth" occupied a stall that had once been meant for a horse. There were two other cows so accommodated in the stalls next to her; clearly the stable was being used as a dairy, but there were horses housed here still. They were absent at present, but he could smell them. He took a slow breath, letting the scent fill him, knowing that this, at least, was something with which he was familiar.

"Mr. Wakefield, shall you delight us with your expertise, or shall you stand and reflect?"

He started and focused on the slim woman before him, still standing rigidly erect, but now with her head tipped inquisitively to one side.

He cleared his throat and took the bucket. "I cannot promise delight," he said.

"Milk shall be enough."

He was not going to evade this test, so he might best be done with it. He turned and looked at Elizabeth, who eyed him mildly over the stall door, peacefully chewing her cud.

"I usually bring her out to milk her," Miss Dearborn said, "but the straw is clean if you prefer the stall."

Since this was something he could do, he led the cow out and tied her in the alley between the stalls, conscious of his audience. Then he picked up the pail again and looked at Elizabeth.

Elizabeth looked back.

He approached slowly, stopped, and then set the pail down carefully beneath her udder. He straightened and gazed at it, then turned around, scratching his head. He caught sight of Miss Dearborn, watching him silently, and she raised her arm and pointed at the stool, which rested by the near wall. He retrieved it, placed it by Elizabeth and sat down.

Now what? Miss Dearborn clearly expected a performance, but to perform he needed to know where to begin.

Visions of a young girl milking flashed through his mind. The teats had to be squeezed. She also had to be uncomfortably close to the animal to do it, for he remembered her head resting on the cow's flank. He hoped his own arms were long enough to forgo that aspect of the process.

He leaned in and took Elizabeth's near front teat. It was warm and rather limp. He squeezed.

Nothing happened.

He reasoned that he should try a different teat. He squeezed the far front one, and again there was no milk. He ducked his head down a little and looked. A fly buzzed by his ear, and Elizabeth's tail lashed across his face. He jumped, bounced his head off Elizabeth's side, and landed on his backside on the hard brick floor.

"What is the matter?" asked Miss Dearborn. Her voice quivered. He thought—no, he *knew*—she was trying not to laugh.

"I do not know. I think she has no milk." Wakefield got up with as much dignity as he could muster and righted the milking stool.

"Of course she does—unless someone has stolen her milk in broad daylight!"

Miss Dearborn appeared close at his side and crouched down beside his feet. He felt her warmth every bit as much as he felt Elizabeth's, and he stopped breathing.

Miss Dearborn reached beneath Elizabeth, took one teat in hand, and immediately a thin stream of milk spurted into the bucket.

Miss Dearborn stood up and stared pertly up into his face. "She has milk."

"I think she does not like me."

"Nonsense. You just need to try harder."

He set his jaw. Miss Dearborn stared right back at him, a twinkle lurking in her gold-brown eyes. He was foolish to think he had to do this, but he refused to be shamed. He sat down on the stool, seized Elizabeth's teat, and squeezed hard.

The next thing he knew, he was lying on his back

on the stable floor, with Miss Dearborn leaning over him. His side felt as though it had been hit with a cannon ball.

"What did you do?" demanded Miss Dearborn. Her voice sounded rather breathless.

He drew an excruciating lungful of air. "I? I did nothing. It is your beast who has done something."

"Elizabeth is not a beast!"

On his other side, Joseph chose that moment to prod at Wakefield's ribs. Wakefield gasped, drew up his own hand, and grasped Joseph's wrist.

"Do not touch me again—or I shall kick harder than that ruminating she-devil!"

Miss Dearborn made a choking sound, and Wakefield looked up at her pretty face leaning over him. She was not in distress—far from it. Her hand was clapped over her mouth, and her eyes shimmered with amusement.

"I am glad to see that you are concerned with my injuries," he said.

"Oh, bother! Joseph, has he broken any ribs?"

"Joseph cannot experience my ribs as I can." Wakefield ran his fingers over his own side. "I do not think anything is broken."

"Very well, then." She stood and extended her hand, urging him to get up. "She did not kick that hard. Did I not tell you to use a gentle hand?"

Wakefield got painfully to his feet and then stood rubbing his aching side. The "beast" looked quite innocent, regarding him with a particularly placid, cowlike expression.

"Forgive me, Miss Elizabeth," he said, "but I have just acquired a taste for a nice roast of beef."

"Oh, for shame!" cried Miss Dearborn—and then,

she laughed aloud. Wakefield turned to see her glee-
ful face, and even old Joseph cracked a smile.

"I think," said Wakefield dolefully, "that I cannot
milk a cow."

Miss Dearborn shook her head, still giggling. "Oh,
dear. I do think you are—right. I do not think it—
possible for anyone to—*pretend* incompetence so well!"

Annabelle instructed Angus to accompany Lizzie to
the stable for the following morning's milking, since
she had no better solution. As much as she had been
unable to tell the household that Mr. Wakefield had
been the milk-and-egg thief, she could not tell them
that the thief had been caught, as clearly this was not
the case. Wakefield could not be her villain.

She had truly suspected as much as soon as she had
seen him in the library, however, and perhaps earlier.
Oh, she knew that he was a gentleman's son, but gentlemen's sons were sometimes poor, and sometimes
desperate. They were even sometimes scoundrels.
This was something she knew very well, for it was a
gentleman scoundrel who had cheated Father out of
what little that remained to them. But Wakefield was
different. He was not the sort of gentleman whose situation would have reduced him to learn such a thing
as how to steal milk.

That his only sin was in being attacked and robbed
himself now seemed quite clear, but he appeared no
closer to remembering who he was. And that led to
the next difficulty.

To the larger portion of the household, Wakefield
was . . . Wakefield. He was a man with a memory, a
man who was recovering at his leisure from a carriage
accident. Only Annabelle, Joseph, Bottom, Thistle,
and Angus knew the truth. But since "Wakefield" was

a "guest," he was having dinner in the dining room tonight. He had said that for him to remain eating in his room would be to arouse suspicion, now that he was clearly fit; and with that, Annabelle had had to agree.

This, however, necessitated she tell Mother all.

Annabelle found her mother in her little sitting room, lying on the chaise and gazing languidly at a book. She looked up curiously as Annabelle entered.

"Yes, what is it, dear?"

Annabelle sat down and composed herself. Mother's gaze remained upon her, as though she knew something momentous was about to be revealed.

Annabelle took a breath. "Mother, Mr. Wakefield is not 'Mr. Wakefield.' He cannot remember who he is."

Mother stared blankly at her for a moment. Then she closed her book, turned on the chaise to face her, and sat up straight.

"Mr. Wakefield cannot remember?"

"That is right." Annabelle continued rather rapidly. "It is clear he is a gentleman, but more than that we do not know. A blow upon his head seems to have put everything out of it. We are hoping he will remember soon and all will be well, but in the meantime—"

"Heavens, why did you not tell me before? How fascinating! A mysterious gentleman!"

Annabelle stared at her mother in surprise.

"Do not sit there and stare at me like a goose! Tell me all!"

Annabelle let out a breath of relief. "Mother, he has no money, you recall. He was robbed."

"Of course he was robbed. You have done the correct thing. How did this happen?"

"He does not remember. He awoke injured and with no memory."

"That dratted road, with every creature imaginable traveling upon it! But who would have thought it would be good for something? I should like to meet Mr. Wakefield. I have had nothing to entertain me so in an age."

Annabelle refrained from mentioning that Mr. Wakefield could not share her mother's enthusiasm. For that matter, neither could Annabelle. The man was . . . disturbing to her, and not in a way she could explain to Mother.

"He will be having dinner with us tonight with the other guests. You have had the headache today, so you will not be down, but—"

"Not be down? Nonsense! Of course I shall be down! I will not miss this for anything!"

Annabelle took a breath. "But you must be very careful when you speak to him, for the guests do not know of his . . . difficulty. They believe he is Mr. Wakefield."

"Do they? Well, I cannot think of a reason they cannot know. Hush! Do not worry. I know how to guard my tongue."

Mother had surprised her. First, by not being angry, and second, by being so aroused by curiosity that she decided to come to dinner tonight—something she never did on days she complained of the headache.

Annabelle left her mother, praying that *she* would not get the headache that had apparently abandoned her mother. But while the headache remained at bay, Annabelle's nerves were in high form. Would Wakefield be able to cover his lack of memory? Would Mother inadvertently reveal him? What on earth would she do if the ruse were discovered? She could not afford to lose her only two paying guests!

The time for dinner came. Mr. Goodfellow arrived in good spirits; Captain Morgan hobbled in with his cane, his thin face drawn in customary pain, and stood like an old warhorse resting one leg. Mother was next. She swept in wearing violet silk, a lace fichu at her neck fastened by a large amethyst brooch, her arms draped in a figured India shawl.

Annabelle had just that moment to consider this surprise, as it was the first she had seen her mother out of black. The next surprise quickly superseded it. Wakefield entered.

He had changed. Thank God he had changed; she had no objection to that. But he had changed more than his clothing. He was different.

Wakefield had apparently gone deep into Father's wardrobe and found something from Father's more slender days. He wore knee breeches and an old-fashioned cloth coat with brass buttons. Annabelle might have been amused if the outfit did not suit him so very well; it was an excellent fit, and moreover, Wakefield wore it as if it were every bit as correct as the newest thing. Not by expression or movement did he betray any discomfiture; he glided into the room as though he belonged, nodded to the gentlemen, and immediately made his bow to Mother and offered to seat her.

Mr. Wakefield, whoever he might be, had instantly endeared himself to Mother. Annabelle watched her mother gaze at him in patent approval. Truth be told, Mother's cheeks gained a flush of color, and she smiled in pleasure.

"I would be very pleased," Mother said. As Wakefield seated her mother with perfect good grace, Annabelle looked at what her mother saw. It could have been the resurrection of Father's youthful figure, but Annabelle saw that it was more. Together with his manners and carriage, Wakefield made a very fine-looking man.

It was Annabelle's turn to be seated. She accepted Wakefield's assistance with what she hoped was perfect calm, although she scarcely felt so. She saved her next glance at her mystery gentleman until after all were settled.

Mother was at the head of the table, with Wakefield to her right as she had requested. Annabelle sat at Wakefield's right hand, a measure to protect him from unwanted conversation; Mr. Goodfellow and the Captain sat opposite. In a moment Annabelle ascertained that Mr. Goodfellow's main concern was his food as usual, and the Captain's the difficult placement of his stiff leg. At this juncture Annabelle glanced at Wakefield.

He was attractive. No, he was handsome. From her angle the bruising that lingered could not distract her, and she saw only the strong, classic lines of his solemn profile. His dark hair, neatly tied back in a short queue, allowed an even stronger impression of his face. He looked self-possessed and dignified. Moreover, his table manners were not merely excellent; they were impeccable.

Annabelle felt her awareness of him growing and inner warmth that bespoke a feeling that surprised . . . and alarmed. He was *someone*. His conduct was much too good for one of the lower gentry. He was someone, God forefend, to whom she was attracted. And yet if he were indeed *someone*, she must trust him less than any man she had ever known.

What was Mother saying to him?

"Things were so very different before my dear Mr. Dearborn's last illness. He was so very proud of Hartleigh. His grandfather, the admiral, had acquired it, and Mr. Dearborn considered it his ancestral home. Admiral Dearborn had a remarkable career, you know. He captured many valuable ships, and one in particular—oh, and I forgot the name! But it was famous for the prize money it paid."

"He must have been a great boon to the navy."

"Oh, he was. My husband was so proud of his father. And he did so love his horses. My husband, that is! He had a beautiful pair of grays, and we would go for a drive on exceptional days in the spring."

"I am very sorry for your loss, Mrs. Dearborn." Mr. Wakefield spoke with quiet sincerity, yet there must have been something more in his look, for Annabelle was surprised to see a tear sparkle at the corner of her mother's eye. Mother rapidly banished it.

"One cannot mourn forever what is done and cannot be changed. But what you see now—it is not the Hartleigh that was once. And now my daughter does the duty of a housekeeper and maid! You must not think she was brought up to that. She had the most excellent prospects. Annabelle was once engaged to the heir of a viscountcy."

"*Mother*," Annabelle whispered urgently.

Her mother looked at her and raised one brow. "You protest my plain speaking? It is only the truth. There is hardly a thing to be lost by the telling of it."

Annabelle gazed at her mother, astonished at her mother's unusual loquaciousness, and with a stranger, no less.

"I am a horseman myself," said Wakefield. "I should have liked to see the grays. Does any of your husband's stable remain?"

Annabelle forgave him then for hearing what she hoped he would not, as he was clearly sensible of the delicacy of the topic and was steering it to firmer ground. But wait—he recalled he was a horseman?

"Sadly, his best are gone, but we have horses for the fieldwork and the necessary travel. Clearly we cannot keep expensive animals. You have only to look at our dress. I am sure you have seen the latest thing in London, and here we are in our old things."

Mother must be ill. Annabelle, more and more alarmed, stared at her mother's face and felt the flush on her cheeks was not excitement, but fever.

"We do not know if he has been in London, Mother."

Wakefield turned to look at Annabelle, and something in his eyes projected quiet reassurance. He looked back at her mother.

"I have been in London, but I am afraid I take little notice of very fashionable ladies. Loveliness to me is an altogether different thing." He paused, and then said, "There are no ladies in London who are lovelier than yourself and your daughter."

Mrs. Dearborn beamed in happiness. Annabelle laid down her fork, having suffered a complete loss of appetite. Not only was she mortified, she was terrified that her mother would now remark on Mr. Wakefield's apparent memory.

"I agree!" said Mr. Goodfellow. "They are splendid ladies, both of them. I do not like London ladies by half. Betimes, you cannot tell a lady from a—well, that is to say, one cannot tell a lady by her gown and hat feathers."

Annabelle's humiliation was now complete. She had one other concern than ending the meal as soon as possible, and that was to see her mother to her room and getting her to bed. Mother was not herself.

The ordeal lasted a bit longer. Miraculously, Mother did not ask Mr. Wakefield about his memory of London and ended the meal at last. Leaving the gentlemen at table, Annabelle followed her mother upstairs.

"There is nothing the matter with me!" her mother protested as soon as they were safely in her chamber. "You are such an odd child! You are at one moment set against the most reasonable request, and now you are following me as if I am dying! I am perfectly well. Thistle, take my shawl."

Annabelle stood still, helpless as Thistle began readying Mother for bed. There was no point in dismissing Thistle if she would listen at the door, and Mother would refuse to have her evening routine interrupted in any event.

"Are you certain you do not have a fever, Mother?"

"I am tired. That is all. Why would I not be?"

Mother sat at her dressing table, and Thistle began letting down her long hair for brushing. Mother gazed at herself in the looking glass and smiled softly.

"This Mr. Wakefield," she said, "is an interesting gentleman. He is from very good stock, if I do not miss my guess. Imagine, dressing in Mr. Dearborn's old clothes so he might properly wear knee breeches to dinner! He did just as if Hartleigh were a grand estate. That, and he did not look like a figure of fun! I should think no other man could have done it."

Annabelle gazed at her mother's reflection, at her soft smile by candlelight. Since Father's death, Mother had looked every one of her forty-odd years and more; but tonight, Annabelle thought she had never looked so young, or as pretty.

"Yes," Annabelle said quietly, "he does seem very much the gentleman."

"Thank goodness you noticed. I should have lost all hope for you if you had not. And do you know, I cannot help but believe he has come here for a reason! Not of his own design, but by fate's. Why, I do believe he will help us out of this muddle we are in. I believe he is the man you are to marry, Annabelle!"

Chapter Six

Wakefield had seen little of Annabelle for several days now. This was for the best. He had feelings for her that were not proper given his situation, and regardless of what hers might be, his presence seemed to cause her discomfort. He was, then, glad for the chores he was given to perform by Joseph, who seemed to have decided to trust him.

The thief was the cause of his least favorite task. Due to the three milk cows being confined to the stable at night, he had been given the unenviable job of cleaning the stalls after them. It was something he definitely was not used to, but unfortunately, it took little instruction.

The boy who worked for Annabelle, Dick by name, was very happy for his company. Previously the stall cleaning had been his job, and Dick was delighted to share. In turn he told Wakefield most of his simple history. He had been born down the road a way; his father was in the navy, he did not know where; his mother was a laundress in the village; his surviving sister was married to a farmer and had three children. His job was to help with the sheep at lambing time, do any other odd jobs that Joseph gave him to do, and bring the cows to the stable at night and take them to the field in the morning since the milk stealing began.

Dick liked to talk. This was fine, for Wakefield did not. Still, even though he would not have chosen the job, he was beginning to find a simple satisfaction in a job well-done.

He did like learning new things. Scything and trimming the hedges he found to be relaxing, although the first day resulted in bleeding blisters on his hands. He wrapped his hands in strips of cloth and continued diligently, taking pride at the results of his labors. Angus, who had previously been responsible for all the outside work, had clearly been somewhat negligent—but as Angus was now working in the field at the spring planting, Wakefield could not think ill of him.

Agricultural toil produced a strange soothing effect. Perhaps plowing would be to his liking. And at odd moments when his mind was quiet and engaged in the rhythm of his movements, pictures flashed through his mind.

The wind was in his face. He was hot and sweaty and far too long from a decent bath. He was tired and hungry besides. But he rode on with no thought of rest. . . .

Wakefield lowered the scythe and stared unfocused into the distance, trying to recapture that fleeting memory, but nothing more came.

"Halloo! Me papa be 'urt! You got to come!"

A raggedy lad came running across the grounds toward him, stumbling with fatigue, his eyes large with fear. He staggered to a stop in front of Wakefield and began his appeal once more.

"Hold, hold," Wakefield said. He settled his hands on the boy's thin shoulders. "What happened? And where?"

"T' ox got stung, 'e did, and took off w' de plow and me papa. 'E went down an' fell on 'im. I'll take you."

Wakefield was already harnessing the only available horse to the wagon when Annabelle came running into the stable with Dick.

"What are you doing? What has happened?"

Wakefield interrupted the farmer's boy, who began his explanations again. "The boy's father is hurt. Said the ox fell on him."

Annabelle did not hesitate. "I am coming."

"Where is Joseph?"

"He has gone to check on Angus in the field."

They said nothing more. Wakefield quickly finished harnessing Annabelle's Molly to the wagon, and shortly he was beside Annabelle on the seat with the boys behind. Wakefield took the reins.

"You need to drive quickly," Annabelle said. "Do you know if you are a skilled at this?"

Wakefield set Molly in motion. "Yes."

Their destination was not far. With the boy directing them, they arrived at the scene of the accident in good time, considering their pace was slowed by hillocks and a spot of low ground that was too wet to drive through. When they crested the last hill, Wakefield spotted the plain thatched cottage in the distance, the plot of worked ground, and the place where the land sloped downward sharply. The boy directed them there.

Then he saw the situation. The ox had fallen at the bottom of the slope and entangled its hind legs in the traces. The ground was soft due to a recent heavy rain, and it had not been able to gain purchase. The farmer was beneath it, his legs pinned by the trapped animal. Wakefield leapt from the wagon.

Annabelle's midsection tightened in fear. It looked

very bad indeed. She watched from the wagon, wondering if she should go for Joseph and Angus, for poor John Becker was alone with just his wife and young son, with no one else nearby to come. In the distance she spotted John's wife, Sara, coming from the cottage, carrying a bucket and a bundle under one arm, hurrying as fast as she could over the rough ground.

Annabelle looked back at Wakefield and the boys. She saw the boys at the ox's head, holding it as still as they could, and Wakefield was cutting the traces to the plow. She made her decision and started the wagon toward Sara.

"Miss Annabelle!" Sara cried.

Annabelle brought the wagon to a stop and waited while the stout woman climbed in with her supplies.

"I'm so glad you come. My John—oh, Lord, 'e's hurt, I know 'e is, and if 'is leg is broke, I don' know what we'll do. Billy can't do it alone. Oh, Lord above, help us."

Annabelle felt her heart breaking. The Beckers had so little and worked so hard. They had been on this piece of land for years, and had suffered all—the death of their eldest son in the army, their daughter's death in childbirth. Annabelle had reduced their rent as much as she could, but her own resources now put her at a stand.

Annabelle turned the wagon and headed them back toward the accident. "Try not to worry, Sara. We will have John safe soon."

They were empty words, and Annabelle knew it. Sara gave silent testimony, and when Annabelle looked at her, Sara's face was pale and grim.

She heard Wakefield shout and realized he wanted her.

"Bring the horse!"

She arrived with Sara and got down from the wagon. Wakefield immediately unfastened Molly's harness from the wagon and led her down the slope to the head of the ox. Sara hurried down the hill and knelt by John. Annabelle stopped short, waiting and watching for when she might be needed.

Wakefield somehow fastened Molly's harness to the ox's head and commanded the boys to be ready. Then, he slowly began leading Molly forward. Molly advanced a few steps and then hesitated at the resistance as the ox threw its head in panic. Wakefield pulled on her bridle, urging her on. Slowly Molly took another step, then another, straining, her neck outstretched, under Wakefield's guiding assistance.

"Push! Now!"

The boys and Sara, standing over John, pushed hard on the ox's side. Annabelle hurried to join them. Leaning all her weight against the ox's flank, she pushed with the others.

Slowly, slowly, the ox rolled. Annabelle pushed harder, and her light shoes slipped in the mud.

"Miss Dearborn! Get away from there!"

Annabelle stumbled backward, but it was not because of Wakefield's angry shout. It was because the ox suddenly lunged. With the combined strength of Molly pulling and the boys and Sara pushing, the ox gained its feet. John was free.

Annabelle sat on the slope and watched as Wakefield checked John over, feeling his limbs, asking him questions. John cried out in pain. Sara in turn gave John gruff reassurance and made him sip a cup of water.

Wakefield stood then, but only to command the others to find what he needed. "I need two stout, straight branches and some lengths of cloth. Sacking will do."

John's leg was broken. Annabelle's heart fell. She watched Sara stroke his head, over and over, as the boys dashed off on their errands. Wakefield went after Dick and took over the cutting of the limb the boy had found, and presently John's boy came running with an old sack.

Annabelle got up and joined Sara at John's side. John's face was pale and damp with perspiration, his lips pressed tightly closed against any sound of pain.

"Miss Dearborn, I need you here by me," Wakefield said. "John, I am going to straighten your leg, and then tie up the splint. It will hurt."

"I kin stomach it."

"It's not a bad injury. It's clean, no skin broken. You'll just have to be laid up until it heals."

"Can't. Got to plant."

"Someone else will plant. Miss Dearborn and Mrs. Becker, you must hold him as still as you can."

Annabelle clutched John's arm. When Wakefield took hold of John's leg, John cried out and lurched up. Annabelle immediately found herself no match for John's strength, and Sara threw herself across him.

"John, you keep still or I'll make you sorry you're alive!"

John cursed. Annabelle added her weight to Sara's.

"I'm already sorry!" John bellowed.

Wakefield, positioned at John's foot, made one hard pull. John howled. Cringing in sympathy, Annabelle turned her head away from John's face. Now she had a clear view of Wakefield, and watched him deftly splint John's leg and wrap it tight with strips of sacking. In only moments, but moments which seemed to last forever, it was done.

Wakefield stood, and Annabelle sat up. She sat beside John breathing hard, her heart racing, her nerves ragged.

She felt a light touch on her shoulder. Turning her head, she saw the extended hand, strong and reassuring. Gratefully, she placed her hand in Wakefield's and allowed him to pull her to her feet.

"Are you all right?" he asked.

"I?" She took a deep breath and looked up to meet his troubled eyes. "I certainly should be. It is not I with a broken leg."

"You are trembling."

His large hand wrapped hers in gentle warmth, and the steady hold of his gaze unsettled her. Her heart fluttered in agitation. She chose a show of bravado.

"That," she said pertly, "is female nerves. Poor Sara has them, too, but she is better at hiding them."

"I don't have time for nerves," growled Sara. "When I do, I'll take them out on John."

John groaned. "Talk. Talk. All ye do is talk."

"Let's get you home, John, and Sara will get you a cup of something to help the pain," Wakefield said.

Wakefield released Annabelle's hand. For an instant, it felt as though she had lost a lifeline—but then his attention was back on John as though the contact had never been. Taking herself sternly in hand, she looked for a way to make herself useful.

With their arms about John's shoulders, Sara and Wakefield helped John up the slope, while Annabelle ran ahead to spread the blanket in the wagon. Together they lifted him into the back, and Sara climbed in after him to make him comfortable.

Wakefield reharnessed Molly to the wagon, Annabelle climbed up beside Wakefield, and the boys jumped in behind with Sara. In minutes they arrived at the Beckers' cottage, and shortly John was tucked up in his own bed with Sara fussing over him and John insisting that he had to finish the plowing.

"Not 'til after you've had a hot cuppa!" was Sara's stern reply. "A *long* time after!"

On the drive home, Annabelle's heart was full of both gratitude and worry. That John had not been more seriously hurt had truly been a gift, but for a time at least he could not work in the field. This would mean hardship for the Beckers. Her head reeled so with this that she thought of nothing else until they arrived home, until Wakefield handed her down from the wagon. It was with that brief contact that she became aware of him again, and she was very conscious of him at her side as they walked into Hartleigh Hall.

She sought something to break the tension and turned to him in the hall. "I will ask Bottom to make us some tea."

Wakefield met her eyes. His face was smeared with mud, and so was the rest of him. He looked as disreputable as he had ever looked.

Even with her worry and nervousness, his state made her smile. "You are a sight. You had better not let Bottom see you."

"Hm. Perhaps you should come with me." He stepped past her and started up the hall.

"Why?" She followed, her curiosity piqued, her heart jumping just a little bit faster.

"Stop here." He halted by the looking glass that hung over the hall table. "Now, look."

She turned, saw her own reflection, and gasped. Then she burst into laughter. She dashed the stray hair from her forehead, and her fingers left another streak of mud behind.

"I am a fright!"

"Well put. But you are a brave and valiant fright."

His simple statement startled her. She glanced at him, not knowing how to respond. Strangely she wanted to weep, and she could not let herself weep. She spoke quickly to cover her confusion.

"Oh, well, that puts a better face on it. But if Mother sees me, she will have an apoplexy."

"I propose this. If you would be so generous as to have the tea provided, we can meet in a half hour. Will this do?"

Annabelle gazed at him, and her heart quickened at the humor and kindness in his eyes. "Very well." She smiled.

She very much looked forward to that cup of tea.

Once in her room, Annabelle took off her loose work gown and washed her face and hands. She selected a blue flowered cotton gown, slipped into it, threw a shawl over her shoulders, and crossed the hall to Mother's room to have it fastened.

Mother was reading a book of verse and directed Thistle to attend to her, which Thistle did wordlessly. Mother then gave Annabelle a critical eye.

"Can you not find something other than that old gown? And whatever have you done to your hair? Thistle, do her hair. I cannot have my daughter go downstairs looking like a heathen."

"I was about to fix my hair, Mother."

"I have to suppose you came upstairs looking like that. How could you possibly allow yourself to be seen in such a state?"

Thistle finished the last hook and picked up the brush.

"There was a problem this morning. John Becker had an accident, and I went to help."

"You went to help? Are you a man to attend such things?"

"No, Mother. But there are few men here."

"That comes as no news to me. Would that things had been otherwise! But it cannot be, for my daughter is a poor spinster."

Annabelle bit her lip. Thistle set the last pin in her hair.

"I must go, Mother."

Annabelle escaped and was three steps toward the stairs when the mist came over her eyes. She blinked and walked on.

She did not allow one tear to fall.

They sat in the overgrown garden on the lip of the old fountain, not so very far from the hedge where Wakefield had once plucked the rose for Annabelle. The fountain base was of lichen-covered hewn stone, the water within long since still. It was silent but for occasional birdsong, and the clouds that had threatened had scuttled to reveal the warming sun.

"I hope you do not mind taking tea here." Annabelle glanced at him over the rim of her cup. "I suppose you would like the comfort of a proper chair, but I do love this spot. It is very soothing."

"Ah. So I see." Wakefield thought of no more to say. He was full of the moment, of the peace, of the scent of lavender wafting from the woman seated so near him. He gazed at the pink blush of a new rose bloom in the tangle of brambles nearby and felt the dampish breeze that stirred its petals. It would face a gale, he thought, and remain untorn by the thorns. And he thought of Annabelle.

"I have no idea at all what you are used to, or I should know how to deal with you," she said, her tone lighter than before. "Perhaps you should be in the parlor in the big armchair, with your feet on a stool and a footman at your beck and call. Or perhaps you are used to country inns and public rooms, eating a trencher of the evening's stew."

She amused him with her little game, in spite of the twinge of pain her words brought. "I should rather think neither."

"Perhaps you are used to good plain fare served by your wife," she went on. "Perhaps you have a living somewhere and a nice little cottage."

"You would still have me a man of the cloth?"

"Could you not be? You have the education and the mien for it."

She was serious now, and he was too weary to engage in a discussion of his memory or his possible status in life—particularly the idea that he might have a wife waiting for him.

"Ah, but I could as well be a traveling cardsharp. Clever rascals, they; they make their living by appearing to be what they are not."

He gazed at the dainty cup in his hand. It was of pale porcelain with tiny painted flowers and birds, and it made a strange contrast with his large, work-roughened fingers.

"I do not think so. You are too good." She paused and took a sip. In a moment she went on. "I am very grateful to you for helping John Becker today. You did not hesitate. Should your instincts have been otherwise, I should have known. And you knew just what to do."

He looked at her. Her clear amber eyes held his, questioning.

A thought, like a lightning bolt, struck him through.

"It was rather like freeing a mired gun carriage."

Her face opened, soft and delighted, like a flower. "Oh! You remember!"

He drew in a breath. "No. Only that. I—I have had several visions of it." He paused. "I was a military man. I may have been in Spain."

"Of course. It seems so perfectly right. And I have had the good fortune to have you at hand."

He hesitated, gazing at her lovely face. "If only I could be a much greater help to you."

"Oh, but if you could . . . I know . . . oh, dear."

Wakefield was surprised when she turned her face away. Nonplussed, he waited, but she did not look back.

"What is the matter, Miss Dearborn?"

She shook her head. "Nothing."

"Clearly there is something bothering you."

She shook her head again, then lifted her hand, and deftly wiped an eye.

Women. He had never known quite how to talk to them, except as correct manners dictated, and how to console them was much more delicate. How he knew this was beyond him, but he did.

"I do understand that financial worries have been bearing you down. I have unhappily added to your burden, and I wish you to know that I will someway repay the debt. When I leave, that shall be my uppermost thought."

Good Lord, she is weeping. He felt a panic setting in. "Miss Dearborn." He reached out and lightly touched her shoulder. She was trembling.

"Yes, you shall go." Her voice wavered. "I know. And I—I shall go on."

"Miss Dearborn."

"Somehow, I shall."

"It is but the excitement of the day's events. Things will go better now."

"I shall have to help the Beckers somehow, but I don't know how—"

"Miss Dearborn—dear Miss Dearborn—"

She turned toward him on the stone seat, and naturally and simply, he gathered her into his arms.

Chapter Seven

She was a chrysalis, a butterfly enclosed in a golden cocoon. The sun from without warmed her, and the warm breeze stirred her hair; but the sun was his warm body and strong arms, and the breeze, his soft breath.

She did not know how long they stayed that way. She only knew that while he held her, with his strong heart pumping beneath her ear, she was not alone. Her world held someone else, someone who stood beside her and fended off the foes who threatened.

"Miss Dearborn."

His voice was soft but insistent. His arms loosened around her. With a pang of regret, she drew away from him.

"I am very sorry," he said. "Please forgive me."

She sniffed and gave him a stern look. "Why are you sorry? You did not kiss me." She wished he had. It was an odd thing to think of, but she had finally met the man by whom she wanted to be kissed, and he had not done it.

"I—I just feel that I . . . That is, I took a liberty, perhaps."

Wakefield seemed uncertain of himself, and that endeared him to her even more.

"Perhaps you mean you did not mind my weeping all over my father's coat so very much. I forgive you that." Her voice quavered at the end, and that considerably vexed her.

He hesitated before replying. "Yes. Yes, I suppose that was it." He paused. "It is a very good coat."

She wanted to laugh, but the devil of it was that she wanted to cry, too, and if she laughed, she would inevitably end up doing the other.

"Perhaps," he said, "if you told me about your troubles, I might think of a solution."

She gazed at his face, a face that was becoming more handsome by the day with the fading of his bruises. The cut on his forehead was healed but for a thin red line, which a lock of hair could easily hide. She realized then, given what she had learned of him, that this man could easily be spoken for. But for now he did not know.

She pressed down on the place within her that wanted to wail, to protest the bad fortune that kept matching her with men who would not stay. But it seemed to be her lot in life; if it was to be so, then she must make use of them while she could. For the present, she had Mr. Wakefield.

She sighed and gazed about the overgrown garden, lovely in a way for its very wildness. Wakefield would likely begin his work on it soon, and she was certain he would make it presentable once more; but she would miss this one. If he could help with her finances—how, she did not know—she knew she would *not* miss the worry.

"Father was not a wealthy man," she said. "He never was, I think, only I could not know for years.

His money came from his father, who was an admiral in His Majesty's Navy, and who did very well for himself." She paused, looking for a respectful way to explain her father's problem. "My father was an optimistic man. He trusted easily. He was—he was imprudent, and very dear to me, and had a heart of gold. I was eighteen years old when he lost everything. He was devastated."

"How did it happen?"

She stared at the tea leaves in the bottom of her cup. The memory was still painful.

"The last venture was a diamond mine in Brazil. A gentleman convinced him that it was an easy fortune if Father leapt upon the chance and invested with him. Father gathered the funds he could, and for the balance he mortgaged Hartleigh."

"There was no fortune, I gather."

Annabelle looked at him, expecting to see disdain in his eyes—or worse, pity. But she only saw attentiveness.

"No. No fortune. I doubt there ever was a diamond mine. But Father had been convinced and entered the bargain, and once done, there was no undoing it."

"And who might this gentleman be whom your father trusted so much?"

"Perhaps I shouldn't—" Annabelle drew a deep breath. "Oh, what matter can it be? He is Lord Ridlington. And Lord Ridlington also holds the mortgage to Hartleigh."

Wakefield's brows drew together, and his expression became absolutely thunderous. "The scoundrel!"

Annabelle gazed at him in surprise at the vehemence of his remark. "You must understand—I do not know for certain he is a thief! These are thoughts of my own. I have no proof, only unhappy suspicion."

An awareness came to Wakefield's eyes, and he visibly relaxed. "I beg your pardon," he said. He lowered his head and rubbed his temple. "I seem to have ... associated something with the name, but I fear it is a trick of my mind. It is gone now."

"Oh, now *I* am sorry! I eternally forget that you cannot remember. It must be terrible for you, and here I am pouring out all my problems."

"Do not be sorry. I am interested and want to help if I can. And you have scarcely told me *all* your problems."

"I have told you enough, I fear." She looked away from him, not knowing what to do with the intimacy between them, something that was more than an embrace between acquaintances. Revealing herself had made it so. She felt vulnerable and foolish.

"You have told me about your loss of fortune. But I do wonder why you are caring for all of these people."

Wakefield watched her, wondering what it was about her that possessed him so and knowing it was useless to deny it. Sensible or no, he wanted to know more about Miss Annabelle Dearborn. He wanted to help her. He wanted to be with her. He prayed that she would answer him.

She straightened her shoulders. "Captain Morgan and Mr. Goodfellow pay their way. There is only the Comtesse who does not."

"Hm. I can think of a milkmaid who refuses to milk, a boy who is too young to be of much use but receives generous remuneration, and a manservant who spends more of his time sleeping than working— and who has periodic recourse to a flask. And then, of course, there is me."

She did not answer this time, but there was no

point in her explaining why she had made the choices she had. He knew why she had made them. She was compassionate and generous to a fault.

"I should think your mother would be more involved in the running of things. Forgive me, but she seems not to recognize the difficulties you are in."

She drew breath. "Mother knows. She simply prefers not to acknowledge them. She is a baron's daughter, and her life was different than mine."

"Is there no one you might turn to?"

Annabelle sighed. "Well, as to that, my only remaining connections are my mother's. Her father cut her off those many years ago when she married my father, and she has been on terms with no one but her sister since. My aunt is married to Lord Holden of Kent, and they are quite well-to-do. Still, Mother and my aunt see little of each other, and I feel that Lord Holden discourages my aunt from much contact. So there you have it; we are quite alone."

"Why did you not marry?"

Annabelle gasped, jumped to her feet, and rounded on him. "How dare you ask me such a thing!"

He blinked. He had expected a reaction, but nothing compared to this fury. "I beg your pardon. I should not have done."

"How could you even desire the answer? I have nothing but a mortgage for a dowry, and since I have not lately turned water into wine or stone into bread, the question is so foolish it is beyond bearing! *Who* worth having would marry me?"

"I am very sorry. You are right; it was a very foolish question. And inexcusably boorish. I cannot think how I came to ask it."

In truth he did not, for now he saw just how callous

he had been. But it was too late to make amends. Miss Dearborn was untouched by his apologies.

"Give me your cup. I shall go in. You may stay if you like." She walked away with a kind of outraged dignity, porcelain tinkling at every step, and he was left alone in the garden to ponder what he had heard, and what in the world he could do for her if ever he remembered who he was.

"Wakefield, I have an unhappy task for you."

Annabelle stood before the desk in her father's study, rearranging the papers that lay before her. Wakefield saw at a glance that they were bills. She stood very erect, staring at the papers, and did not look up at him. She was at the very least still sensitive to him.

"The thief has returned. One of the cows was found to be milked dry this morning—by someone so bold as to creep into the stable at night. The henhouse was raided as well, and this time a hen is missing."

"Someone is clearly desperate. It seems a guard is needed."

She looked at him at last. "Precisely. I need you to sleep in the stable." She held his gaze, as if anticipating reluctance.

"Then I shall willingly. We shall capture this thief and be done with him."

She looked relieved. "I would want no one hurt, including yourself. It would likely be enough to frighten the thief away."

"No, we must have certainty. I am fully capable, Miss Dearborn. Have no fear."

She sighed, and her shoulders relaxed. "I do hope this person is not dangerous."

"If you have a pistol, I will have it with me."

"There will be no need of it, I am certain!"

"I should not use it unless necessary. I am accustomed to firearms, Miss Dearborn."

She gazed at him, anxiety and deliberation in her eyes. "Do we know for certain you can shoot a pistol?"

"I am as certain as I am that I draw breath. But I shall demonstrate if you wish."

It happened then that the two of them walked out into the windy field behind the stable that morning, Annabelle clutching her pelisse together, Wakefield carrying the pistol case. They paused at last in a slight hollow somewhat protected from the wind, and Wakefield lined up some fist-sized stones along the trunk of a fallen tree.

Annabelle waited for him at the selected distance, and he walked back to join her.

"If you hit one of those, I shall deem you expert," she said.

He stood at his ease beside her and loaded the ball into her father's pistol. "An expert finds a way not to shoot," he said, "but is ready if he must."

"Of course. But that is of no use if he cannot hit anything."

Wakefield tapped the powder horn gently with his finger and tipped a small amount into the firing pan of the pistol. "True." He closed the frizzen on the pan and raised the pistol at arm's length, taking careful aim. He squeezed the trigger.

The first stone flew to the right.

"There. I am satisfied," Annabelle said.

"I am not. That was a glancing blow." He had already added ball and powder. He closed the pistol and raised it again.

The second stone split, and chunks of it tore through the branches of the nearby oak.

"I should think that meets your standards."

"Miss Dearborn, there is a stone remaining."

"How foolish of me. Of course there is."

He raised his arm again, aimed, and squeezed the trigger. The third stone exploded into bits.

"That is all," he said. "I am done."

Annabelle sighed heavily. "I am glad. I am chilled through."

He packed up the pistol, and they began walking home. He felt tension emanating from her, unrelenting still.

"You could as well be a highwayman as a soldier," she said.

He smiled, knowing she could not see him, for she was in front of him, staring straight ahead. She was forgiving him.

"It is possible, of course. But if I am a highwayman, I must be a devilish poor one. What self-respecting highwayman would be seen behind John Becker's plow? But today, I shall place myself in just that position for the amusement of all and sundry."

She laughed. And the sun broke through the scudding clouds.

That night as he lay in his straw bed in the stable, when he was tired and aching from a day in John Becker's field, he thought of his morning with Miss Dearborn. The wind . . . the smell of black powder . . . Annabelle's laugh. It was a strange combination, Annabelle together with the echoes of his unremembered past. But in an odd way, it seemed to form a link between his past and his present.

As for his future, that remained an unrelenting blank.

Annabelle. How could he allow himself feelings for her when he had no idea who he was, what he possessed, and most alarming of all, whether or not he was free to choose? He might be promised. He might be wed and the father of young ones. Yet nothing in his urgency to remember told him if that might be the reason for his haste, or if there was something else entirely that drove him. *Remember. Remember.* It was like a drumbeat in his head, and yet to attempt it was like seizing a cloud.

Thank God he was so tired. He closed his eyes, but still he could not rest. Annabelle filled his mind, and he remembered what she had told him earlier. Her father had gambled all and lost, ending all hope of a marriage—and likely ending the engagement her mother had mentioned. And her father had been swindled, so it seemed, by a Lord Ridlington.

His body tensed with anger. He rolled to his other side, then to his back, and stared blindly in the dark.

He did not know why he was so angry—whether it was with Ridlington for cheating an honest man, or with Annabelle's father for gambling away the family's fortune. A gentleman might inherit, but he also inherited his duty as the head of the family, and he must shepherd his fortune for the welfare of all whom he protected. How could Mr. Dearborn risk all when a wife and child depended upon him? Now they were left in a precarious state and faced a life of poverty. There was simply no excuse for that sort of behavior.

Eventually Wakefield realized that his teeth hurt from clenching them. This realization led Wakefield to examine himself for the root of his anger. For some time he grappled with the shadowy images in his mind, images that danced just out of reach; and just as he was about to admit defeat, the face of the old man appeared.

You are no son of mine.

Wakefield sat bolt upright. His heart pounded in his ears; he could hardly draw breath.

The old man, his face livid with fury, shook his finger at him. "You are no son of mine. I wash my hands of you."

A cold sweat broke out over his body. He did not know the man's name, but he knew who the man was.

The man was his father.

Annabelle lay in her canopy bed, the draperies parted so she could see the play of moonlight as it slipped across her floor and crept over the counterpane that covered her. It was cool in spite of the clear sky, but as she was under many layers of coverings, she felt it only on the tip of her nose. Mother would disapprove and predict illness from the dreadful night air, but Annabelle had never found it troublesome. It gave her peace.

If only it did so tonight—but its soothing touch could not seem to mend her tired spirits. She felt more disheartened than usual. Since her father's death, she could not remember feeling so, as though there were truly no hope. And somehow her feelings were tangled up in the mysterious form of Mr. Wakefield.

She had developed an attachment to him, and in a way she had not felt before. Her feelings for Mr. Harwell had been . . . different. She had been but eighteen and completely naïve; she now knew what insincerity could hide beneath a charming manner and an appealing face, and such had been the case with Mr. Harwell. But in Mr. Wakefield, she had seen much more than the charm and the face. She had seen a man of principle, a man of integrity. She longed enough to wish, by some magical means, that it would be possible for them to marry.

For this wish, she would find her heart broken. Many were the possible reasons that Wakefield would eventually leave her.

"Father," she said to the empty room, "you see how things are. Mother is useless and I am at a stand. I need a sign—*another* sign, if you please—but this time, do not send me to the stable to find a naked man in it!"

She closed her eyes and tried to imagine her father's response other than the one thing she remembered him to say often: "Do not fret, my dear. We shall come about."

Through the open window came the loud report of a gun.

Chapter Eight

*H*e awoke as lightly as a feather falling to earth. He lay in the darkness, listening, instinctively quieting the beat of his heart and the sound of his breath. As still as the stable was to his ears, he was certain he could hear a mouse blink; and so he continued to listen for the sound.

There it was: a stealthy tread, and one that would profit from being a good deal more quiet. Slowly Wakefield sat up and felt for the pistol at his side. Now he would have some action!

He had chosen to bed down in one of the empty stalls, under the cover of a dark blanket, so he would not need to attempt the creaky ladder in the inky blackness. He listened again, hearing another soft sound and the cow stirring in her stall.

Wakefield carefully crept through the stall opening into the alley. He could not see, but the sounds had told him the intruder was in Mary's stall, a good choice for one bent on theft as the old cow was startled by nothing.

He crept to the doorway of the stall. He had no light, but by listening, he knew the thief was intent on getting milk and not on avoiding discovery. Inching forward, he made out the soft white glow of Mary's flank and the shadow hunched below it.

He launched himself at the intruder.

Annabelle leapt from bed, snatched up her dressing gown, and frantically sought her slippers. *Wakefield had fired the pistol.* Worse still, perhaps the pistol fired had not been Wakefield's! Her mind screaming in panic, she raced from her room only to collide with another in the hall.

"Miss Dearborn!"

"Joseph!"

Joseph stood before her holding a lamp, dressed in his green silk dressing gown and his boots.

"Miss Dearborn, I must ask you to go back into your room!"

"I shall not!" She pushed past him and raced toward the stairs.

"Miss—" Joseph broke off and came sprinting down the stairs after her. Annabelle reached the front door paces ahead of him, but Joseph intervened and unfastened the locks, which he could perform more quickly in the dark than she.

"I shall go to the fore," Joseph said.

They set off for the stable at a run, Annabelle falling behind due to the uncooperative nature of her slippers, not because she meant to oblige Joseph. Joseph reached the stable door and pulled it open.

"Joseph! Be careful! Someone might be—"

Joseph had already slipped inside.

Annabelle picked up her skirts, let the offending slippers fly where they might, and ran after him.

When she arrived, breathless, Joseph stood in the stable alley, holding the lamp high so the light fell into Mary's stall.

"Are you harmed, Wakefield?" he asked.

"Yes," came Wakefield's voice. "The smell is choking me."

Annabelle dashed to Joseph's side and stared down into Mary's stall. There, beneath the belly of the placid cow, lay two entangled figures. One, whom she determined to be Wakefield in the dim lamplight, had a strong hold of the other. Of the other she could make out little but that he was gasping for breath.

Knowing Wakefield was safe was the greatest possible relief, but she immediately had another concern. "You fired the pistol!" she cried. "You have hurt him!"

Wakefield grunted. "Thank you for your concern, Miss Dearborn, but I did not shoot him. I took pains to miss him."

Annabelle stared at the two figures in the straw, her eyes adjusting to the dim light. "Why did you shoot at all?"

"I wished to gain your attention, and it appears I was successful. Have you more questions?" Wakefield sounded exasperated, and Annabelle held her tongue.

"Can you endeavor to bring him out here, Mr. Wakefield?" Joseph asked. "I shall hold the pistol, if you would so kindly indicate where it is."

Joseph handed Annabelle the lamp and entered the stall to retrieve the pistol. Wakefield then struggled from beneath Mary, holding his now-unresisting prisoner. When Wakefield and Joseph at last brought the intruder from the stall, Annabelle was surprised to see an old man dressed in a very dirty suit of clothes.

"Who are you?" Annabelle asked.

"I ain't hurtin' nothin'," the old man whimpered. "I'm hungry. Just a'ter a bit to eat."

"You are a thief," snapped Wakefield, holding the

old man securely by the back of his collar. "You have been terrifying this household."

"You might have come to the door," said Annabelle, "and asked for food."

Wakefield released the old man and took the reloaded pistol from Joseph.

"I do not tolerate thieves," Wakefield pronounced sternly. He stepped into the circle of lamplight.

At the sight of Wakefield, the old man's eyes widened, and he seemed to shrink into himself. Annabelle was not surprised. The look Wakefield gave the old man was quelling in the extreme, and Annabelle was glad it was not focused on herself. But she found she had not truly appreciated the reason for the old man's fear.

The old man swallowed. "I didn't mean nothin'! I didn't hurt you none! I needed the clothes. All I done is take your clothes!"

Wakefield stared at the old man, dumbfounded. For a moment, all were immobile with surprise. Then Annabelle held the lamp closer.

The suit was slack about his thin form. It might have been a good suit of clothes, but now it was nearly impossible to tell.

"You were there when I was attacked," Wakefield said grimly.

"I only saw what they done from the bushes," the old man protested. "They throwed you off a wagon and took off down the road. I come over, and then I figured you wouldn't be needin' the clothes. I thought you was a goner!"

"What is your name?" Annabelle asked gently.

The old man looked at her. Suddenly, the last remnant of his bravado was gone.

"Kyne. Jamison Kyne," he said wearily. "I ain't got

no kin. I lost my farm, and I can't get hired on. Too old."

Her heart went out to him. Perhaps the saddest result of partitioning was the effect on old men like Mr. Kyne, who lost the plot his family had farmed for generations. Without livelihood and too old to be wanted elsewhere, he was doomed to wander, penniless.

"Mr. Kyne, would you like to come to the kitchen for something to eat?"

"Miss Dearborn—" Both Joseph and Wakefield spoke at the same time and then looked at each other.

"Do not listen to them," Annabelle said. "It is no trouble to spare you something to eat. And perhaps we can think of some way you can be of service."

Annabelle was very aware of the silence from Joseph and Wakefield behind her as she led Jamison Kyne to the kitchen. Neither would let her be alone with Mr. Kyne, and Mr. Wakefield carried the pistol in plain view. She decided to ignore them.

If Mr. Kyne was telling the truth, and she believed he was, he still had his farming skills. She knew where they could be used.

Rather than waken Mrs. Bottom, Annabelle went to the fireplace to rebuild the fire; seeing what she intended, Joseph wordlessly took over the task, and Annabelle slipped out to the larder to find what was left for an impromptu meal. When she returned, Joseph had the fire burning, and Mr. Wakefield still stood grimly on guard, holding the pistol.

The poor old man looked so hungry that Annabelle ladled him out the stew before it was fully hot and cut him thick slices of bread. The three of them stood around the big kitchen table watching him eat, which he did with great enthusiasm.

Mr. Kyne sat back at last, having cleaned his bowl with his bread and devoured the last piece. "This is lovely," he said. "Lovely, indeed. I can't think when I last had a good plate o' stew."

"Then you were due for one," Annabelle said. "Now, we must talk."

"I have something to say," said Mr. Wakefield. "I would like my clothes returned."

Annabelle cast him a disapproving look. It should have made him ashamed, but Wakefield merely stood there glowering.

"I think that Mr. Kyne has got the last use of them," she said pointedly.

"He apparently has. Such being the case, I suggest you give him some clean ones."

"Oh, an excellent idea," she said, immediately mollified. She had not misjudged Mr. Wakefield after all, regardless of how displeased he was. "Of course."

"What ideas do you have for Mr. Kyne, Miss Dearborn?" Joseph asked.

Poor Joseph! He was put out with her, she knew, every bit as much as Mr. Wakefield was.

"I think he could help the Beckers. There is too much for Sara and their boy to do alone. I will provide his meals, which is a small thing for me to do, and the Beckers will have their planting done in time." She paused, assessing the expressions on the three male faces in her kitchen. None appeared happy but for Mr. Kyne, who looked hopeful.

"You have work?" he asked. His voice quavered a little, and he seemed to be afraid to believe his good fortune.

"Yes. A farmer nearby has an injury and needs help with his planting. You can sleep in my stable. The farm is only a short walk from here. Would you consider it?"

Mr. Kyne gave her a toothy smile. "With pleasure, mum! I'm sound, I am, and I can do a good day's work. I ain't big, but I got heart. All's I need is somethin' t' eat."

"Very good, sir! Then we are settled. Joseph will show you where you can wash up and sleep, and I will send you some clean clothes. As to what you are wearing, it appears Mr. Wakefield would like it back, so you may leave it in the stable for him."

She turned to Mr. Wakefield then. "And you, sir, may go wash up with Mr. Kyne. I will not have anyone in my house smelling of cows!"

The only good outcome of the night, as far as Wakefield was concerned, was that he was to be allowed a real bed once more. He was not convinced that Mr. Kyne was an honest man, but Miss Dearborn would have her way, and he hoped there was no livestock missing in the morning.

Then again, a deep instinct told him that Miss Dearborn was right about the old man. Kyne was a victim of hard times, and for that Wakefield saw the justice of charity. He had to give Miss Dearborn credit for her very generous heart—the same heart that had shown charity to another destitute stranger less than a fortnight ago. It was something he was determined never to forget.

Miss Dearborn was a different kind of female from those he had known—and notwithstanding his lack of memory, he most assuredly had known women. None, he was quite sure, would have given of themselves as Miss Dearborn did, with a kind heart and genuine compassion.

There was one thing that plagued him about Miss Dearborn, however: It was his memory of her in her flimsy housecoat, barefoot, holding the lantern above her head. There was one brief moment when he had mistakenly stepped slightly behind her, and although he had corrected that error with all possible speed, the memory of her slender form in silhouette was indelibly impressed upon his mind.

It was in all likelihood the reason he had been so hard on the old man, for he had been dealing with a very uncomfortable case of frustration.

A few buckets of icy-cold water over his head in the stable yard did much to remove his unpleasant aroma as well as the complication Miss Dearborn had inadvertently caused. Wet and shivering, Wakefield reentered the stable to dress and retrieve the filthy suit of clothes from the old man.

The old man was already snoring, and Wakefield walked softly to keep from waking him. In a few minutes he found the discarded pile of clothes and gathered it up.

They smelled ghastly, and not just from a roll beneath a cow. Wakefield bundled them into a sheet to minimize the aroma and crept back into the house.

Once in his room, he carefully opened the bundle and examined the items one by one: a man's cotton shirt, formerly white; a pair of very grimy doeskin trousers; a black cloth coat; a soiled gray waistcoat. There were no fobs or suchlike, not that he expected anything of that nature to remain, but he most regretted his missing boots, which must have been sold. But there was something, and it gratified all his hopes.

A tailor's label.

*   *   *

When Annabelle arose the next morning, she found that Wakefield had risen before her. She rightly guessed that he had gone to the stable and taken Mr. Kyne to the Becker farm, which Joseph confirmed, so she went about her morning duties more cheerfully than she had in weeks. With the good fortune of capturing the thief and getting help for the Beckers in one fell blow, she had hopes of her luck turning.

She had to laugh at that thought. How like her father she sounded!

She arrived at Mr. Wakefield's room at last in her task of gathering linens. The odor that met her at the door told her that all was not well. In a moment she found what she expected: the pile of filthy clothing that had been taken off Mr. Kyne.

She stared at it, exasperated, and yet something touched her deeply. Mr. Wakefield wanted more than anything to remember, so much so that even these dreadful remnants of his clothes were precious to him.

Dropping the armload she carried, she began lifting the articles of clothing, examining them closely. They were well-made, she saw. They were what she would expect a gentleman to wear, be he a man of business or of a loftier position. It was a pity they were ruined. Was there anything she could do to restore them at all?

She tucked them into her bundle of bedclothes, still considering her options, and continued with her morning's chores.

She did not see Wakefield again until later in the day, when he returned from the Beckers'. Her spirits lifted when she saw him from her parlor window—riding in upon the prankish Jezebel no less, so he must have let Mr. Kyne borrow Molly that morning.

She watched him a moment as he slowed Jezebel to a walk at the top of the far rise and easily held her to that gait as they approached the stable.

She could add horsemanship to the growing list of Mr. Wakefield's talents, then. And *would* her foolish heart stop swelling and fluttering at such nonsense!

She doffed her apron, however, and quickly flew to a looking glass. Her stray hairs patted into place and the smudge wiped from her chin, she picked up a cloth and began aimlessly dusting the wall sconces in the front hall as she awaited him.

The door opened, and Wakefield strode in with a puff of fragrant breeze. He looked fresh, she thought, invigorated—no longer exhausted as he had on his first days of toil. Even in simple laborer's clothes he looked dignified, although the thought was likely the product of her heart's bias.

"How are the Beckers?" she asked.

"As well as can be expected. John has come through a spot of fever, and his leg appears to be mending." Wakefield doffed his hat.

"And Mr. Kyne?"

"He does very well," Wakefield said. "Clearly born and bred to farming. Pray excuse me, if you will."

"Of course."

He headed up the stairs to freshen himself, and Annabelle had to be content with that for the moment. She did not wait long. Less than a half hour later, he found her in the kitchen garden where she was weeding parsnips.

He came up behind her where she knelt, and she sensed his presence by a prickling in her spine.

"Miss Dearborn—"

"Oh, Mr. Wakefield!" she said without looking up. "I have been thinking that the hedges need improving in the formal garden. I have grown used to the wild look of it, but after all, it is not quite seemly. Since you are not required to help Mr. Becker now, I thought perhaps you could do this as your next project."

She happily pulled another weed and then noted the ominous silence from Mr. Wakefield. She looked up.

Wakefield stood there in clean trousers and shirt, his hair still damp from his recent ablutions, a look of strain on his face.

Annabelle rose to her feet and pulled off her soiled gloves. "Is something wrong?"

"My clothes. They have been removed from my room. I realize they seem worthless to you, but I have reason to save them."

"Oh." She poked a strand of hair back beneath her cap. "I am sorry. I took them to see if I could clean them."

He sighed in unreserved relief. "Thank you. I should like to save the coat if I can. It bears the mark of my tailor."

The significance of this struck Annabelle before Wakefield finished his next sentence.

"I shall need to go to London as soon as I may. I must find this tailor, and God willing, discover who I am."

Chapter Nine

*H*e would leave her. She had known it; she had
been right. Her foolish hopes! And here they
had all depended upon a man whose past was a mystery, who might very well be an impoverished
younger son or some such, a man she once would not
have considered for a husband.

She had changed, but the world had not.

She stood there in her kitchen garden, clutching her
soiled gloves in her soiled apron, a wisp of hair tick-
ling her forehead instead of being properly tucked
under her cap. Quite likely she was a sight—and suddenly, it mattered.

"Miss Dearborn?" he asked.

"Yes. Yes, of course."

He studied her face until she glanced away and
pretended to watch a hawk circling at some distance.

"I had meant to make a request. It is that I—I have
no means of transportation, no funds to sustain me
for the journey. I do not want to ask for your help, but
if you could assist me in this, I shall repay you just as
soon as possible."

Annabelle looked at the ground, fighting for composure and to stave off the pain in her breast. When

he found this tailor, he would indeed learn the truth. What would it be? Would he be married? Would he be someone of high rank, beyond her touch? Would he be an ordinary gentleman, free of ties, who would return to her?

At last she sighed and looked up.

He appeared uncomfortable, as a man did when forced to do something that was completely against his principles. Clearly he would do anything to learn the truth about himself.

"You must go. It is the only hope you have, and my only hope of ever . . . ever being repaid." She drew a deep breath. "I am most pressed at this moment. Until the harvest is brought in, we are quite poor, and even then we may not do."

"I am sorry. I am imposing too much. I shall find another way to London."

"No, no. I am considering my own position, and now it seems that . . . I really must sell Father's ring."

Annabelle lifted her hand and carefully retrieved the ring, which hung from a ribbon around her neck. Gazing at it, she saw again how it glowed like a sunrise when the light hit it just so; and she remembered when her father had placed it in her hand.

"It was Grandfather's. It came from a Spanish cargo, and he could never bear to part with it."

"Miss Dearborn, you must on no account sell it on my behalf."

She glanced up sharply and caught the expression of concern in his eyes. They were very dark and very soft.

She swallowed. "I shall not. I am simply facing a truth. I must sell it to go on, and so I shall. I shall accompany you to London."

The gentle breeze brushed by them then, cooling

her damp brow and stirring her skirt. It was as if, she suddenly thought, her father approved her plan.

"It would not be proper," Mr. Wakefield said.

"Of course it shall be. I shall bring Joseph."

"He is needed here."

"Oh, will you stop being so obstinate!" She was suddenly in a pet and wanted nothing more than to flounce off like a schoolgirl and have a good cry alone; but there was no acceptable way to do this, so she dropped to her knees in the vegetable bed and put her gloves on again.

"I am not," he said. "I am being reasonable. I cannot think of only myself."

"You need not think of me, for I am quite able to think for myself," she snapped. She pulled furiously at the weeds. "So I am informing you that I am going to London to sell my ring, and you may accompany me if you wish."

He was silent for a moment again. At last he said, "Very well. I shall not trouble you more at the moment. There is no need to decide all at once, in any event. We shall speak on it again."

He departed, and Annabelle was left to wish she had said this, or done that, and to agonize tearfully over the hopelessness of it all.

"Of course I shall go to London!" Mother exclaimed. "You cannot possibly go without me. It would be improper in the extreme. Besides, I have a wish to see my sister, and I cannot think where else you could stay."

Mother was in a rare surge of enthusiasm, examining a half dozen gowns Thistle had laid upon her bed, while Thistle had been dispatched to retrieve even more from storage. Mother held up a violet satin with a black net overskirt and gave it a critical eye. "The waist must come down a bit. A band of ribbon might do the trick; and the sleeves must be redone. Annabelle, you must look at your gowns."

"We do not have time for renovations, Mother."

Mrs. Dearborn laid the gown upon the bed and turned a sharp eye on Annabelle. "You cannot go to London looking like a country bumpkin. I will not allow it. You are nearly two and twenty, and an opportunity as this cannot be cast away!"

Mother picked up a rose silk next, held it up, and frowned at it.

"I will hold it for you, Mother." Annabelle took the dress and held it up for examination. A speculative look came into her mother's eyes.

"This gown is too young for me, but it is perfect for *you.*"

"Mother, we are not of a size! You are taller than I am."

"This is why women were given needles and thread, my dear."

Thistle arrived with another armload. Annabelle held up another gown, then another, while her mother passed judgment. When Thistle brought bonnets, Annabelle made her exit, leaving her mother pulling off trims and demanding her sewing box.

Annabelle was relieved. She couldn't go to London without Mother, and not only for the need of escort. Mother knew London and knew its ways. Mother would also ensure them a place to stay at her sister's townhouse. Mother and Aunt Holden, Lady Holden, had little to do with each other given their different stations in life; but Mother would have her way regardless of what Lord Holden thought of the matter.

Several days passed since the decision to go to London. As Annabelle went about her preparations, Mr. Wakefield had his own matter to attend.

Wakefield had little to do in the way of readiness on his own account, but he was surprised to receive a request from another. Joseph accosted him one morning and gave him the information that Madame la Comtesse wished to see him. Puzzled and curious, Wakefield climbed the stairs to Madame la Comtesse's room.

The old woman servant in black met him at the door, and he entered. He had never seen Madame la Comtesse, and was not prepared for the picture that met his eyes.

Madame sat regally upright in a voluminous sack-backed gown of purple taffeta, her bodice boned and tightly drawn around her thin body. She wore a tall white wig with a black cap perched atop it, and lace cascaded from the cuffs of her long sleeves. In her lap she held a curiously carved wooden box.

Madame had a lean face, a sharp long nose and dark snapping eyes, and she held him in an unflinching stare.

"Vous êtes Monsieur Wakefield, est ce vrai?" she asked.

He made a polite bow. Then he answered with amazing ease. *"Oui, ce vrai. Je suis charmé, Madame. Comment est-ce que je peux être d'aide?"*

Madame blinked. "Ah, so we may converse in French! However, we need not. Thank you for calling, Monsieur Wakefield. I do have a favor to request, as you have guessed."

"Certainly," he answered. At the moment he had lost all curiosity about her request and was preoccupied with his ability to speak French.

"But first, a question. Do you recognize me, Monsieur?"

His attention immediately returned to the Comtesse. "No, I do not, I am afraid." His heart leapt.

"Ah, very good. *Non*—I can give you no information. I have no more idea who you might be than you know who I might be. But there was a chance." She paused. "Of course, Monsieur, I do understand your particular problem. You remember nothing. Are you surprised? You should not be. I have a way of knowing most everything. Do I not, Celeste?"

"Indeed," said the old servant, who stood motionlessly by, awaiting her lady's command. Wakefield thought of a stuffed raven with watchful eyes.

In fact, the entire room was odd—quaint and old and motionless, like the two women within it. The window curtains were open, allowing the morning light, and that was the only thing that seemed alive.

"I understand you will be going to London," she said.

"Yes."

The Comtesse opened the box in her lap and withdrew a folded paper, sealed with a wafer.

"You are a gentleman of honor. As such I entrust this task to you. I require you to call at 16 St. James's Street at the Bank of Sir Robert Herries and Co.; there, you should ask to see Mr. Farquhar and only he. It is to him you must give my letter. He will follow my instructions and return a packet to you, which you will bring to me. You must promise your absolute confidence in this matter. Do you agree to assist me?"

Wakefield considered a moment. At last he said, "I cannot see a reason I may not do as you ask. A business errand is a small matter to attend to on your behalf."

The old Comtesse nodded. "Very good, Monsieur. Do have a care, however, to remember my instructions. See only Mr. Farquhar, and maintain strictest confidence."

"Agreed."

She handed him the folded paper, and he slipped it into his coat pocket. "Is there anything else?"

"No, there is not. I shall await you, then." Then she smiled. "Ah! It is so comical that I endeavor to escape my past while you attempt to discover yours! Life is rather like a game, Monsieur, which is played by fate. When you are a bit older, you will understand."

They traveled slowly to avoid the cost of changing horses, with Wakefield serving as coachman, and arrived in the late afternoon at Lord Holden's residence on Hertford Street. Annabelle nervously followed her mother into the hall, not knowing how they would be received, while Mrs. Dearborn seemed perfectly self-possessed.

They were directed to a parlor just down the hall and to the right, and were left to wait. Annabelle gazed at the ornately carved sideboard with its display of crystal and wondered how long they would be allowed to cool their heels. Presently steps were heard, and the door opened to admit her aunt Holden.

Mother arose. "Hello, Caroline."

They exchanged perfunctory kisses, and when Annabelle's turn came, she curtsied politely. Aunt Holden nodded in return.

Aunt Holden was shorter than Mother, plumper, and wore a worried expression on her smooth, round face. The look of worry was characteristic, if Annabelle's memory served her rightly, but this time she guessed that there was more reason for it.

"I have only just had your letter," Aunt Holden said.

"Really?" Mother raised her brows. "I had sent it, oh, a fortnight ago." Of course, she had only sent it three days before, quite intentionally.

"We are rather busy at the moment," Aunt Holden went on, her hands fluttering nervously as she spoke. "I have a soiree planned, and we have invitations for tonight as well."

"I certainly hope we are not an inconvenience," said Mother. "Had we known, we might have changed our arrival."

"Oh—oh, no, not an inconvenience, but I hope you understand. Holden will not wish to interrupt his plans, and our soiree is—ah—rather exclusive, and it is too late to postpone."

Mother smiled. "But that is nothing. Surely your guests will understand a visit from your dear sister and her daughter. We shall not be a bit of trouble! If you will only show us to where we shall stay, we shall get ourselves settled, and then we can exchange gossip. It has been such a long time since we have talked!"

Aunt Holden was powerless against Mother. Annabelle was equally certain that Mother understood very well what Aunt Holden meant to say but could not: that their arrival *was* inconvenient; that they could not be included as guests at Aunt Holden's exclusive function; and that they were very much beneath Lord and Lady Holden in status, however closely they were related. Mother had made the irreparable error of making a poor marriage, while Aunt Holden had made an excellent one. The gulf could not be breached.

Mother was the elder sister, however, and had always been headstrong, and Aunt Holden meek. Mother was never intimidated. And although Annabelle's uncle by marriage was a strict and unbending man, Annabelle had no doubt that Mother would stand up to Lord Holden as well.

They were shown their chambers. While Annabelle unpacked her few things with the help of one of Aunt Holden's maids, she wondered what Mr. Wakefield was doing. He was maintaining his guise as coachman and would not be admitted into the family quarters.

Hopefully, her opportunity to attend to her errand and visit a jeweler would not be long in coming. She wanted Mr. Wakefield with her. She was not certain why, but she told herself it was because he likely had buried knowledge that would help her. But whatever the reason, something warned her that if he found his tailor first, her chance would be gone forever.

Wakefield was experiencing a headache right between the eyes, and as much as he wanted to set out on his errands immediately, he lay down on his narrow bed in the servants' quarters and tried to relax. His room was on the lowest level, not far from the kitchen, and he shared it with a young groom who was thankfully about his duties.

Wakefield found no relief, however. Arrival in London seemed to have stirred up all kinds of turmoil in his head. He had rapid flashes of memories—of streets, of houses, of sensations. He experienced a strong feeling of familiarity when he had driven down a portion of Bond Street, and again on St. James's; and as he had turned a corner near Green Park, he had had a sudden flash of distress, as though he recalled a past danger. Nothing remained with him

so that he could seize upon it and study it, however.
The memories flitted off like shadows, leaving him
with the knowledge he had had them but not with
their substance.

He was near discovery of his identity, he was certain, but what if he *learned* who he was but still could
not *remember*? He wanted it to be over, the awful
gnawing inside his head, the worry, the sudden panic
he sometimes felt for no reason whatsoever. Still, he
feared his memories. Something was not right. He
had left something important undone; someone was
in trouble; and he, himself, was certainly in some sort
of fix. What else, when someone had left him for
dead?

Why would someone *want* him dead? For deep inside, this was what he truly believed. The assault was
not part of a simple theft.

Then, crowning it all was the fear that he had a wife
he could not remember while he was very much in
love with Miss Annabelle Dearborn, his one and true
guardian angel.

Was there any possible way he could put his life
right?

His distress at last settled into melancholy, and he
suddenly could not bear to lie any longer in the tiny,
closed chamber. He would not be wanted any more
today, and he was unable to speak with Miss Dearborn. He arose then with no better plan than to wander the streets of London and perhaps to stumble
upon a miracle.

Chapter Ten

*A*lone in her room at last, Annabelle lay down on the chaise longue to recover from the journey. She was bone weary; however, her mind would not let her rest.

She determined that she must act quickly. They must go to sell the ring at the earliest possible opportunity. They would then find the tailor, and Mr. Wakefield would be free to pursue what he must.

Annabelle felt a certain urgency to convey this information to Mr. Wakefield lest he make plans of his own, and so she arose and went to the writing desk, took out an expensive piece of vellum and composed a note. Then she rang for her maid. Jane appeared in good time, and Annabelle gave her the note with instructions to deliver it as soon as possible.

Jane bobbed a curtsy and was off. Annabelle went back to the chaise longue, relieved that this matter had been dealt with. She was starting to doze off when the scratching came on her door.

At her summons, Jane reappeared.

"I'm sorry, Miss Dearborn," she said, "but Mr. Wakefield is gone."

"Gone? He cannot be gone!"

"But he is not in his room, Miss, and Jeannette saw him go two hours ago and more."

"Can there be a mistake?"

"No, Miss. He is not here."

"Very well, then . . . if you are certain."

The door closed behind Jane. Annabelle, with all peace ruined, stood and paced her little chamber while she reasoned with herself. *He would not leave us now. He has gone to find the tailor, and he will come back.*

Annabelle tired of pacing at last. There was nothing she could do but wait. In all likelihood Mr. Wakefield would return by morning with interesting news, and she would not need to explain that their coachman was missing.

Wakefield walked dejectedly down St. James's Street, amusing himself by watching the small groups of well-dressed gentlemen stroll to and fro, sometimes silent, sometimes laughing at some jest. There were impressive equipages to be seen as well, occasionally with a notable crest on the door. The unappetizing scent of the Thames was ever-present, but somehow less on this exalted street. He looked everywhere for something that seemed familiar, wondering if he belonged here.

He would find the tailor tomorrow; his head throbbed still, and he was unequal to it today. Beyond that, he still wore the dusty clothing he had traveled in. His mind would not be quiet, however.

A sign caught his eye just then: Sir Robert Herries & Co. He stopped and took a folded missive from his coat pocket.

Yes, it was the same address. This was Madame la Comtesse's bank, where he was to perform her requested errand. Deciding to have it done with, he entered the premises.

The young clerk he encountered looked at him askance and inquired about his business in a tone Wakefield recognized, one that was specifically used to keep the "lower orders" in their place. He felt instant resentment.

"I am here on an errand," he said brusquely. "I must see Mr. Farquhar."

The clerk raised his brows. "Mr. Farquhar? I am afraid he is not available. With what may I help you?"

Wakefield set his jaw. "I must see Mr. Farquhar and no one else."

"And who might you be?"

Wakefield caught himself. He did not know the answer. Should he give the false name and hope for the best? But what question might come next? And was it possible that someone might recognize him after he had given the alias?

He cleared his throat. "I am on a confidential errand for a lady, and she requested that I speak with Mr. Farquhar and Mr. Farquhar only. I must beg that her request be honored."

This speech seemed to prompt the clerk to some action, and he left his window and passed through a door behind him. Wakefield presumed that he had probably given the impression he was a servant—no matter, as long as the blasted thing got done.

The young clerk reappeared, looking sullen, and stepped around the counter. "Come with me, please."

Wakefield followed him into a small office. An older man sat behind a mahogany desk, and he looked up from his writing as they entered.

"I am Mr. Farquhar. How may I help you?"

"A private word, if I may. I carry a message for a lady, and she begged complete confidentiality."

Farquhar eyed him a moment, then looked at the young clerk. "You may go, Jones."

As soon as the resentful clerk stepped out, Wakefield handed Farquhar Madame la Comtesse's note. Farquhar adjusted his spectacles and read it. Then he cleared his throat and looked up.

"She says I may trust you. However, I must insist on some satisfaction of my own. How are you acquainted with the lady?"

"I am afraid I would compromise her secrecy if I were to tell you."

"Can you tell me where she is residing?"

"I cannot. That is, I could if I chose, but it is not her wish."

"Hm." The old man stared at him. Then he said, "Her request is rather odd. I wonder if you can describe the lady for me?"

Wakefield sighed inwardly. What had appeared to be a simple errand was not so simple after all.

"She is elderly, tall and frail, with all of her wits about her. As to her request, I can only say that I have no idea what it is, but if it seems odd, I am not in the least surprised. She is a bit of an eccentric."

Then Mr. Farquhar smiled. "Ah. It seems you do indeed know the lady. Very well. Wait but a moment, and we shall be done."

Minutes later Wakefield left the bank with a folded packet in his hand. He took a moment to read the direction written upon it: *To Lady F.*

Lady F? Wakefield pocketed the packet, bemused. Yes, there was a mystery here. He already knew that la Comtesse spoke French with a very poor accent. He might entertain himself with solving her puzzle if he did not have his own to untangle.

He found himself at last in front of a club where some instinct made him pause. The door was reached by mounting several steps, and farther down was a bow window jutting outward. Wakefield frowned, reaching for the vaporous thought. *The door used to be where the window is now.*

Where had that thought come from? And how did he know it?

"White's," he said out loud. *The club is White's.* He stared up at the bow window, groping for more. There were several gentlemen sitting in the window alcove, backlit by candlelight. Did he know them?

"Gregory? My God! It *is* you! I thought they had killed you!"

Wakefield turned sharply. A man was nearly upon him—and then he was engulfed in a powerful embrace.

Wakefield stood, unmoving. In a moment the stranger released him and stepped back.

Brown eyes much like his own gazed into his, frowning. He was a slender young gentleman of much his own height, well-dressed in a good coat, white neckerchief and top hat. He had been, Wakefield realized, on his way into White's.

"What is wrong?" the young man asked. "Where have you been, and why are you wearing those old clothes?"

Wakefield swallowed. "Do you know who I am?"

To this, the young gentleman looked astonished. "You are joking!" He paused. "You are *not* joking."

Wakefield drew a breath. "No, I am not. I do not know who I am—or who you are."

The young man stared. Then he said in incredulous tones, "I am Harry, your own brother."

It was Wakefield's turn to stare. *His brother.* Merciful God, his brother! But look as Wakefield would, he did not know him.

"What is my name?" Wakefield asked.

Young Harry's jaw dropped. Then, he inhaled and straightened his shoulders. "You are Gregory, Lord Swain."

Wakefield hardly knew if he could believe his ears. Lord Swain? And yet it sounded right. "I have a title?"

Harry gave him another long, studying look. "We need to go somewhere to talk."

"Do I belong to White's?"

"We can't go in there. You are the oddest figure imaginable! You can't be seen looking like this!" Harry looked quickly over his shoulder at the bow window, and then clapped a hand on Wakefield's— *Lord Swain's*—shoulder.

"I know. We shall go to my rooms. Quickly—let us get a cab. The sooner you are off the street, the better!"

Harry soon obtained a cab, and some minutes later they arrived at a small hotel off St. James's Street. It was an unpretentious establishment, hardly distinguishable from its neighbors, and Gregory recognized it as a place more known for economy than niceties.

Harry led him inside and up the creaking stairs. They mounted three flights and then traversed a long, dimly lit hall nearly to the end. Harry took out a key and opened the door.

"Come inside. Find a chair—blast, the housekeeper has not been in again!"

Harry hurried ahead of him and removed a coat, a

crumpled neck cloth, and some unmentionables from the most available chair.

"Sit down. I shall pour us some drinks. I am afraid I do not have your preference. I have a nearly undrinkable wine."

"What is my preference?" Gregory sat down, gazing about the small apartment. It sported several chairs, a table, a narrow bed, and a good deal of disorder.

Harry returned with a bottle and two glasses. "You prefer a very good sherry, although perhaps I should not tell you." Harry smiled and handed Gregory the glass, then cleared a chair for himself and sat.

Gregory took a sip and restrained himself from making a face. Harry, watching, chuckled.

"Sorry, old chap."

Gregory took another sip and found it not quite so bad as the first.

"Do I stay here?" Gregory asked.

Harry looked bemused for a moment. "You? Lord, no, and I doubt you could be compelled to!"

Gregory grappled for words, but Harry did not wait for an answer.

"Oh, never mind! I was just having sport with you. You never liked it; you have not been here above twice, and that was when you needed to pin my ears back for something or other."

"I see." Gregory saw, and yet he did not. He did not understand his relationship with this young man who called himself his brother, and Gregory wondered why he would have been angry with Harry.

"Where do I stay, then?"

"In the country, mostly. At Kilburn." Harry paused. "That is your country seat. It is in Derbyshire. But you also have a townhouse on Grosvenor Square."

He had a house in town! Yet nothing was happening in Gregory's mind. He had to keep reminding himself he was *Gregory, Lord Swain*, for "Wakefield" seemed more familiar. He sensed that Harry was very worried, and yet the young man did not seem to recognize the extent of Gregory's loss. Gregory knew exactly what Harry told him and no more.

"I should like to know what happened to you."

Gregory looked up to meet his younger brother's eyes, now direct and grave. The young man looked uneasy, perched on the edge of his chair, resting his forearms on his thighs and holding his glass in both hands.

Gregory cleared his throat. "There is not so much to tell. I awoke naked in a ditch in Leicestershire without a thought in my head—and with a considerable bump upon it. I was rescued and taken in by some good people who have kept me until now. By good fortune my coat was recovered, and knowing the name of my tailor, I came to London to find him."

"And learn who you are?"

"That is correct."

Harry was frowning. "You have no idea who has done this to you, or why?"

Gregory raised a brow. "I suspect I should recall my name before I remember that."

"Perhaps. You might have been set upon unawares."

"Might I have been carrying valuables?"

Harry sighed. "You were on horseback. You had just left Lord Ralston's in Hertfordshire, I would guess, where you had called to—er—extract me from one of my 'harebrained stunts,' as you put it. I left before you to return to London. You had nothing of great value excepting your horse, I should say. You are not an easy man to ambush in the normal way. Eyes in the back of your head."

"What was your 'harebrained stunt'?"

Harry's lips curved into a slight smile. "Pretending to be you."

"To be me?" Gregory stared at him, nonplussed.

"Yes. So I could ensnare an heiress. I am not worth a bean, you know."

"I see." This time, he *did* see. Being poor was a thing he had recently become intimately acquainted with. "I believe there are more practical ways to achieve a reverse."

Harry leaned back in his chair and crossed his legs. "Ah. You have gained tact. Perhaps you have been in want of a bump on the head."

"Perhaps. But now I should like to know some things from you, such as why an heiress would wish to marry me."

"Ah!" Harry grinned. "Well, you are an exalted individual, a lord of the realm, and the lady is an American looking for a British title. You were invited to her welcoming party but did not go. I believe she miscalculated your degree of desperation. In fact, you are decently set these days."

"I am?"

"My dear brother. Would I jest with you about this? I have nary a chance of getting a loan from you unless you believe you have money!"

Gregory breathed deeply and felt his body relax. Here was some good news, laying to rest his fear that any money he may have possessed had gone to debt. He could repay Miss Dearborn for her aid—even offer her assistance. She would not have to sell her father's ring.

"Perhaps you might enlighten me as to my title."

Harry's brows went up. "You cannot recall *that*? You are Gregory Alden Swain, eighth Earl of Swain. You took the title two years ago when Father passed away."

Harry stood abruptly and walked to his back window where he stopped and gazed out at the alley. Gregory watched him, noting how he stood with one knee cocked, how he swirled the wine in his glass. All this seemed familiar to him. And he sensed within a deep sense of protectiveness toward Harry.

"I need to say this," Harry said slowly. "Matters are much more grave than I thought. I am concerned for your mind. I am sorry, Gregory, but I am devilish worried."

Gregory cleared his throat. "If you are that, imagine how I must feel." He paused. Harry did not answer. "Harry, I am not insane. I merely cannot remember. Believe me, no one wishes my recovery more than I do."

Harry sighed. "I . . . I believe that."

"I am certain I will come about," Gregory added, not knowing if this were a certainty at all.

Harry hesitated an instant and then turned slowly toward him. "The matter is, it may not be soon enough. I think you may be in danger—and I believe I may be the cause of it. I think someone had you followed and meant to have you murdered."

Chapter Eleven

The next morning Mr. Wakefield was still missing. Annabelle went to breakfast prepared to give the bad news to her mother, but as events evolved, she was able to keep Wakefield's absence secret a little longer. Mother had resolved that they would sell the ring and go shopping that very morning, and her intention was to use one of her sister's carriages.

"For there is no point in going about in a sad rattletrap when a very fine conveyance is sitting unused," Mother said. "We may even borrow a pair of Holden's horses and let ours rest another day. An added benefit to *you*, my dear, is that you will be seen about town in a good equipage, and all will wonder if we are not in good circumstances. I should not be a bit surprised if some introductions should come of it."

"But, Mother," Annabelle said, "we still have no money. Matters are the same as before."

Eleanor Dearborn tied the bow of her blue satin bonnet and admired her reflection in the hall mirror. "You *must* forever be certain of failure. I sometimes cannot believe that you are my child." She turned around and looked at Annabelle critically. "Hm. You will do. The white spotted muslin is a pretty gown, and trimmed up with the lavender ribbon, it is much more stylish. And with the purple pelisse you appear less a schoolgirl, which you certainly are not."

Aunt Holden had excused herself from the foray, which was little surprise to Annabelle. Thistle and the little maid Jane accompanied them in the lavish chaise, and they were soon off at a smart trot.

Through her little window Annabelle watched the streets pass and remembered happier times. That and the weight of their present circumstances lowered her spirits, and she worried about her mother's planned shopping expedition. Mother would find such things as a bolt of fine silk and ostrich feathers necessities, claiming they had experienced a drought of such items for much too long.

Oh, how I wish Wakefield were here.

The driver brought the chaise to a stand in front of the jeweler's establishment on St. James's Street her mother had decided upon. Amidst the turmoil of carriages and horses and the press of pedestrians in front of the shops, Annabelle and her mother were let down.

Annabelle followed her mother into the shop and waited until Mrs. Dearborn summoned the proprietor's attention.

"We would like you to evaluate an heirloom piece," she said. She looked at Annabelle, and Annabelle stepped up to the counter and presented the ring.

The proprietor took it and then with great care examined it under his loupe. Annabelle waited and at last inhaled when she realized she had stopped breathing.

"A very fine piece," he said.

"It is Spanish," Annabelle replied. "It is quite old."

"Ah, I should say it is. It is a good example for its age. Were you considering having this reset?"

"No," Mother said. "We are inquiring about its worth."

The jeweler looked at the piece again. "Well . . . excellent workmanship . . . and a most excellent garnet in very fine condition."

"A garnet?" Annabelle asked.

"It is no garnet! It is a ruby!" Mother cried. "You are mistaken, sir!"

The jeweler looked at her over the top of his spectacles. "I am very sorry, but it is a garnet. A very fine garnet of exceptional color, but a garnet nonetheless."

"My dear sir, a garnet is not that color of red," Mother protested. "I *do* know a garnet when I see one."

The jeweler held the ring out to her. "I am giving you my professional opinion. Garnets come in a great variety of colors and shades. *This* is a garnet. If you wish, I can make you an offer. If not . . ."

Twenty minutes later they left the shop. Annabelle was silent, too unhappy to speak. Mother was less reluctant to voice her opinion.

"Robber!" she snapped.

Annabelle could only grieve. She would have kept the ring rather than give it up for such a paltry price, but Mother would have none of it. Annabelle had given in.

As for the shopping, Annabelle could not enjoy it at all. Mother was determined upon it, however, in spite of the severe disappointment at the jeweler. Mother insisted on new kid gloves and a shawl for Annabelle. They were to make an excellent appearance at her sister's soiree, Mother said, and Annabelle must be prepared.

They arrived home to find Lady Holden waiting for them.

"What is it, Sister?" Annabelle's mother asked as they entered Lady Holden's private parlor.

"Oh—" Aunt Holden looked up, attempted to smile, and instead appeared faintly sick. "Lord Holden would like to speak with you. If you will sit down, I will let him know you are home."

Mother frowned. "Your husband wishes to speak with me? Whatever for?"

"It will only be a moment!"

Aunt Holden escaped the room, and Mother's frown deepened.

"What is it, Mother?"

"I think you should go to your bedchamber and see if your new shawl properly matches the rose silk."

Annabelle left reluctantly but met Lord Holden almost immediately in the hall. He nodded curtly to her and, passing her by, entered the room Annabelle had just left.

Annabelle hesitated. It was wrong to eavesdrop, but she felt compelled to know upon what subject Lord Holden wished to speak to Mother with such urgency. *Thistle* would not let the opportunity pass by!

Annabelle went quietly to the door and inclined her ear.

". . . very sorry, Mrs. Dearborn, but it cannot be helped. It would be seen as highly irregular. My wife is in no condition to bear the awkwardness it would cause. Surely that is of importance to you."

There was a slight pause—a very slight one.

"Have you any idea how Caroline feels about slighting her only sister because she is expected to do so?" Mother's voice was that slow, icy, haughty tone that Annabelle had learned to fear. "Do you know how she feels to realize she is putting a period to her niece's only chance at an eligible marriage by refusing her sanction?"

"Mrs. Dearborn, you are making this very difficult."

"My husband was an honorable gentleman. He was the son of a decorated admiral in His Majesty's Navy."

"That is all well and good, but your sister married *me*. I am a bit better than the son of an admiral in His Majesty's Navy!"

Silence.

"Mrs. Dearborn, I am very sorry. I should not have said that in such a way. I simply meant to make a point. Caroline and I cannot include you in the invitation. I am certain she is very distressed over this matter—in tears at this very instant, in fact. You must see reason."

"I think," Annabelle's mother said slowly, "that you would do well to inquire as to exactly *why* my sister is in tears—if she is not afraid to say what she feels."

A pause.

"I think we have spoken enough, Mrs. Dearborn."

Annabelle caught her breath, glanced quickly about her, and sprinted on tiptoe through the open door to the drawing room across the hall. She had barely slipped within when she heard Lord Holden's heavy step leaving the parlor.

In spite of Mother's best effort, they were not to attend the soiree. Annabelle would have no need of the rose silk gown and new shawl, and she would not need to suffer through any pointless introductions. Nor would she save Hartleigh, and looming more ominously than ever was her fate as governess.

Annabelle realized then how much her impractical, demanding, critical mother loved her.

The next morning Annabelle's mother briefly explained her conversation with Lord Holden to Annabelle and concluded that the final humiliation would be to beg her sister's husband for conveyance home, and therefore, they would do no such thing. Even more unacceptable was the thought of going home by stagecoach or post. They would wait for Mr. Wakefield.

After this pronouncement, Mother kept to her room and refused to speak with her sister. Annabelle's aunt Holden looked mournful when Annabelle saw her, and spent much time weeping in private. Lord Holden was seen not at all. As for Annabelle, she waited for Wakefield.

After a day of this had passed, Annabelle felt she could not bear waiting one more day; but the second day passed and the third began. Annabelle felt nearly wild with worry and frustration. Mother's tiff with Aunt Holden was one thing; but something must have happened to Mr. Wakefield.

Annabelle had no servant of her own, so going out was not to be thought of unless she borrowed one of her aunt's maids. Desperation drove her to the point.

To her surprise, Aunt Holden was anxious to please and even ordered her own town carriage for Annabelle's use. She also charged Annabelle with the duty of picking up a package for her, but Annabelle felt this was rather to disguise the loan of the carriage as a favor to herself. Knowing how worried Aunt Holden was about displeasing her husband, Annabelle accepted the carriage with gratitude.

The errand done, Annabelle directed the driver to

the address of Wakefield's tailor, which she had learned by heart: Jacob Gurney, 62 St. James's Street. Her heart pounded unmercifully when the carriage pulled up before the small shop. Fighting her desire to call on the tailor herself, she sent the groom within with her note.

She waited, fidgeting. Finally, the groom reappeared and handed her a response. She opened it with perspiring hands.

I am sorry, but no gentleman calling himself Mr. Wakefield has come by. JG.

Annabelle refolded the note carefully and tucked it inside her reticule. Of what to do next, she had absolutely no idea. Wakefield had no money, no knowledge of who he was. It was hard to believe he had fallen victim of foul play under those circumstances. But he had to be *somewhere*.

Unless . . . unless he *had* remembered. And perhaps, in that case, he had considered his acquaintance with a lady innkeeper best forgotten.

She should not be at all surprised, after all, to find herself abandoned once more.

Gregory Swain found himself in the new, but oddly familiar, situation of being dressed by a small gentleman's gentleman who seemed well versed in Gregory's exact requirements. Finchly's only mistake was to suggest some Imperial White powder to cover the healing scar on Gregory's forehead, which Gregory adamantly declined. He noted, however, Finchly's momentary look of confusion.

"Very well, sir. Will there be anything else?"

"No. You may go."

Gregory finished adjusting his neckerchief and gazed at his reflection in the looking glass. The scar was rapidly becoming difficult to see, and he felt it was of little moment. He was more taken by the image of an authoritative-looking gentleman staring back at him.

Again, it seemed right. He only wished he would *remember*. It was especially difficult when one could not remember one's own mother, who waited for him in the drawing room. And yet he recognized this very house. Everywhere he looked were things that seemed familiar, logically placed. He even knew the silver and crystal epergne on the dining room table.

He had procrastinated long enough. He left his chambers and entered the drawing room with the same feeling of anxiety he had felt before. His mother sat upon the settee before the fire, and his brother, Harry, relaxed in a nearby chair. A third person, a lady, sat with her back to the door, conversing with his mother.

Harry spotted him first and rose. "There you are," he said. "I was beginning to wonder if you could find the drawing room."

"It *is* a townhouse," Gregory said. "I should hope I could." He wondered about the strange woman and whether she was privy to his condition. She turned her head to look at him just then, and he had a full view of her slender face, smoothly upswept hair, and rather small hazel eyes. She possessed a regal nose, he noted, one of which a member of an aristocratic family could be proud.

"Lord Swain," she said civilly. "I am very pleased to see you again."

Gregory wondered if she knew he had been missing. He had not met her earlier and supposed she could not be an intimate connection. Certainly it did not show in her words.

"Good evening," he said.

"Why, Gregory," said his mother. "You might address your fiancée by name."

Gregory shot a look of astonishment at his mother, a dignified, silver-haired woman who sat erect in her chair and watched him with frank intensity. He then turned his gaze to Harry.

Harry wore a mischievous little smile, but he seemingly remembered his manners and disposed of it.

"Gregory, this is Miss Abbotsley."

Miss Abbotsley's face grew a trifle more rigid, and her pale hazel eyes pinned him.

"Certainly you recall Miss Abbotsley," said his mother.

"It appears you do not recall we are engaged," Miss Abbotsley said in that cool, even tone. "I do understand that there is reason, however."

"Ah—yes," Gregory said. He advanced, bowed over her proffered hand, and made the motions of kissing her glove. "Please forgive me."

"Oh, there is nothing to forgive," she said, "providing you never forget me again." She paused as he yet held her hand and probed his face with her gaze. "Do I not appear the least bit familiar?"

Gregory cleared his throat. He was damned if he remembered her at all. "Of course," he lied. *Perhaps he remembered her. Yes, perhaps she did seem to be someone he had seen before. But—to be engaged to her?*

Good Lord. *Engaged.* How was he to say good-bye to Miss Dearborn? The lead weight of grief crushed down on his chest.

"Harry," his mother said, "I feel you should take Gregory through the gallery and show him the family portraits. Perhaps he will remember something there."

Yes. Yes, anything to relieve him from entertaining the marble-faced Miss Abbotsley for ten minutes. Anything for five minutes' reprieve.

"You may wish to go as well," said Mother to Miss Abbotsley.

Damn.

"But you should be left alone then," Miss Abbotsley said. "I cannot allow that."

"Do not worry about me. You may help my son to remember."

And so the moments of respite quickly turned into more minutes of anxiety. Gregory mounted the stairs with Harry on his one side and Miss Abbotsley on the other; and he soon discovered how this gallery visit would go.

They stopped before the first portrait.

"This is your great-great-grandfather, the fourth earl. You can see the likeness. There is a better portrait of him at Kilburn, of course." Miss Abbotsley glanced up at him, as though to see that she had his notice.

"Here is your great-great-grandmother. She was a Sponable. The Swains have always chosen their brides with care, and she was from a very long and very old line. You still have the golden tiara she brought into the family."

As Miss Abbotsley led the way to the next portrait, Gregory glanced at Harry. Harry smiled and shrugged.

"Lady Jane was the eldest daughter of your great-great-grandfather. She did not live long after this portrait was finished," said Miss Abbotsley.

Gregory cleared his throat. "Is there anyone here whom I would remember? That would seem the most expedient place to begin."

Miss Abbotsley turned to him. "This is your family history. You have it committed to heart. I see it as very pertinent and very important." She turned and walked on.

Her every movement was done with stately grace, and her face was a porcelain mask. Clearly her motive sprang from duty, if also to instruct him on her excellent qualifications for a future countess. Indeed, Miss Abbotsley was fit to be Queen. He had apparently chosen well.

But he had chosen for a man he no longer was.

They reviewed a copy of his grandfather's portrait, the original of which hung at Kilburn. Also at Kilburn, he was told, was a very large and beautifully rendered alfresco portrait of his grandfather's family, including his father as a child. None of this was important to him, if indeed it once was. Instead, he was possessed by the mantra hammering in his head: *Engaged. Engaged. Engaged.*

They came to the next portrait, a larger one of more recent vintage.

"And this is . . ."

Gregory heard nothing more that she said. He was fixed on the portrait of a stern-looking old man, glaring out of the portrait at him with piercing dark eyes.

His father. *His father.* He *knew* him. *He remembered.*

Gregory stared, locked in mortal combat with the ghosts of his past. It all came back to him in one gigantic piece, with no gentleness, no mercy.

His father had hated him.

"Gregory?"

It was Harry's voice. Gregory shook himself free and turned to him.

"I have had enough of portraits. I need some fresh air. Forgive me." Then Gregory committed the social sin of leaving his fiancee standing with his brother and strode away, rapidly descended the stairs, and let himself out upon the street.

What a damnable mess. Gregory kept a rapid pace, hardly seeing where he was going but knowing very well where he was. He knew *everything* too well now.

His father had been a heavy tippler who had nearly gambled away all. Only Gregory's unexpected inheritance from a great uncle at age twenty-three had saved the family. Gregory had managed to save most of the land holdings, dower his sister, and shepherd his remaining funds into a respectable fortune by dint of hard work and determination. Gregory had refused to allow his father to control any portion of it. And his father had never forgiven him.

It had been necessary, but it was sheer misery. He had at last purchased a commission in the army to escape his father's resentment, and he had been in Spain when the old man had breathed his last.

So here he was. He had done the responsible thing and engaged himself to the Honorable Miss Abbotsley, of impeccable lineage and some fortune of her own. He had continued to manage the family's assets until he had returned them to their former state of ease.

Lastly, he had been compelled to chasten young Harry for a tendency to follow in their dissolute father's footsteps and had extricated Harry from a gambling loss based on fraud. And *then* Harry had pocketed Gregory's invitation to Lord Ralston's country party for Ralston's American cousin, an heiress from Boston set on marrying a high-ranking English title.

Gregory slowed his rapid pace. It was fully dark now, and the streets were quiet; in but a few hours the *ton* would set out in their carriages and begin the madness of attending as many pretentious and over-heated events as possible. He was grateful for the silence.

Harry. Gregory reflected that he had likely driven Harry to his actions. He recalled berating Harry after the gambling incident in which Harry had lost a hefty sum to Ridlington. He'd sent Harry to the country after promising him that his future allowance would be severely restricted. Then Gregory had had to confront Ridlington. . . . Where had he recently heard his name?

The sound of rapid footfalls behind him made him turn.

"Gregory, hold up!"

Harry appeared from the shadows, slowing as he approached and at last coming to a stop before him.

"What is wrong? You have given everyone an awful turn, dashing out like that!" Harry was slightly breathless, and Gregory could tell he was alarmed.

Gregory took a breath and let it go. "All is well, I fear. I seem to have remembered."

Harry stared at him—and then, he grinned. "That's aces!" he said. "Damme, I am so glad to hear that! But why did you go running off?"

Gregory sighed. "One's past is not the most wonderful thing to contemplate."

Harry's happy look faltered. "Oh, come, Gregory, it isn't all that bad. You have bags of money. You're happy as a clam fixing things for the rest of us, and you have an heiress ready to marry you. I don't know how you can find a complaint. *I* can't."

Gregory gazed at Harry's worried face. "Would you like to be me in truth, Harry?"

Harry looked bewildered. "Are you joking with me?"

Gregory turned slowly and began to walk, and Harry walked with him.

"I feel I owe you an apology, Harry. I have been too hard on you. I may have been right, but my methods have been wrong."

"What? If I gamble away my money, you should not be angry? Even *I* understand that."

"I drove you to make a play for Miss D'Eauville."

"No. I *decided* to. You weren't about and I found the invitation. Opportunity presented itself. What better solution to both our difficulties than for me to marry an heiress? You would no longer have me to deal with, and I would have funds."

"I did not see that as a wonderful solution, given your methods."

From the corner of his eye, Gregory saw Harry smile.

"It *was* rather shabby of me. I should not do it again."

"Thank God." He paused. "It would be best if you were in love with your future bride."

Harry's silence told him how surprised Harry was. Gregory thought it best to change the subject.

"Suppose you tell me why you believe someone tried to murder me."

"Damme, you go from love to murder as though from cakes to tea." Harry paused. "I think that because I know what kind of ramshackle fellow Ridlington is. If you went to him to 'take care of matters' as you said you would do, I should think he might have become desperate. It's no small thing to accuse someone of cheating at cards."

"I understand that. And I also know what kind of fellow Ridlington is, which made me all the more disturbed that you played with him. But that is neither here nor there. What makes a man afraid does not necessarily lead that man to commit murder."

"It does when it's Ridlington."

Both men stopped on the street corner and looked at one another.

"What else do you know of Ridlington?" Gregory asked.

Harry raised his brows. "Only what is rumored in the low circles I frequent, which you detest so much. For instance, there was a fellow Ridlington was on the outs with—you probably did not know him, and it does not matter. This fellow was a captain in the cavalry. In any event, the fellow fell in Portugal, and it was said that Ridlington paid another cavalryman to do the job."

Gregory frowned. "And you believe Ridlington may have played the same game with me."

"I think it possible. If Ridlington felt afraid enough, he would have."

Gregory glanced up and down the street. There was no one within hearing distance.

"I, of course, told Ridlington that I knew he had cheated you at cards and that I would see he never received his winnings—and if he attempted to collect, he would pay the consequences. In other words, I would reveal his actions."

"That's all well and good, but I don't imagine you have proof."

"On the contrary. I located witnesses. He does not know who they are, of course. Fortunately there were quite a number present the evening you accepted Ridlington's stakes."

Harry whistled. "That's it, then. I was right. Ridlington wanted you dead."

They began walking again. For several moments neither spoke. Gregory thought, and thought hard.

Ridlington. Ridlington. Of course! Ridlington was the man who held the mortgage on Miss Dearborn's Hartleigh. Ridlington had swindled Annabelle's father!

"Who knows I am alive?" Gregory asked.

After a moment's hesitation, Harry answered. "I can't be sure, of course, but for myself and Mother and Miss Abbotsley and the servants. There are others who may have seen you."

"But it is generally known that I am missing and may have met with foul play."

"Well, not *generally*. We have tried to keep it quiet."

"But Ridlington believes I am dead."

"I should think so."

"He had me followed." Gregory remembered it clearly now. He had ridden out from Kilburn as soon as he had learned Harry had absconded with the invitation. He remembered on two occasions he had checked behind him, warned by the sixth sense he had developed on the battlefield in Spain, but had never seen anyone. Unfortunately he had dismissed his instincts.

He had been on his way home from Ralston when he had been overtaken. Likely, the thugs thought they had left him for dead. Ridlington had chosen his henchmen badly.

"I am sorry," Harry said. "It is all my fault. You might be dead because of me."

Gregory heard the deep shame in his brother's voice and turned to him. "You are not an equal to Ridlington and cannot be held responsible for what he has done. He has had years to practice his treachery." He paused. "It is plain he must be stopped. He has injured too many."

"What would you do?"

"I shall beat him at his own game," Gregory said. "He thinks I am dead and is likely frequenting his old haunts, feeling very secure. My guess is that a ghostly visit will do considerable damage to his proficiency. I shall challenge him to a game of cards."

Harry gasped. "You are mad! You hate cards with a passion! You told me you would never touch them again. You cannot even know how to play!"

"Au contraire," Gregory said. "I learned at my father's knee. He may have gone to his grave hating me, but he was an excellent teacher of games of chance."

Chapter Twelve

"*I* shall not *think* of you advertising for a position!"
Mother stated flatly. "I shall *not* allow it. A daughter of mine shall *not* go into service. How could you even think of such a thing?"

Annabelle sat with her mother in the small morning parlor, where fortunately they were alone. This was one time that Annabelle especially did not want Thistle to overhear.

"There is nothing else I can do," Annabelle said quietly. "Father's ring brought a pittance, and there is little else save the furniture that is not yet sold."

"You can do better than governess." Mother was as upset as Annabelle had ever seen her. In fact, she seemed astonishingly close to tears.

"Mother . . ." Annabelle reached over and touched her mother's hand. "Aunt Holden cannot help me, even if she would. Lord Holden will not allow it. Therefore there is no chance of an advantageous marriage for me."

Mother looked sharply away and stared out the window. She blinked once but did not reach for her handkerchief.

"I had such hopes . . ."

"I know, Mother. I did as well."

"Did you? I should not have known it."

Annabelle felt ashamed. Her mother had deserved more kindness from her.

"I did, although I perhaps hid this from myself. I thought something would turn up. I have a bit of my father in me after all."

Mother sighed. "I actually had hopes for Wakefield. I felt he would discover himself and find it possible to come to our aid. I actually thought—oh, never mind. But you see, you have not been any sillier than I have."

Annabelle squeezed her mother's hand.

"I think Wakefield will not return," Mother said.

Annabelle thought she was right.

In a moment, Mother spoke again. "Still, I will not hear of you considering a governess position. We are not done yet, and so we shall not bow in defeat until we are."

With this last dictum in mind, Annabelle took out Aunt Holden's carriage to run another errand for want of something to do. With her spirits much depressed, she almost missed a sight that changed everything.

It happened as she was exiting Madame Laurier's Millinery Shop on Bond Street. Her arms were full of packages, as were the maidservant Jane's, and as they emerged, Annabelle looked up and down the busy street for a sign of their carriage, which had been circling the block while they shopped. Annabelle did not see their carriage, but she saw another one.

It actually wasn't the carriage she noticed so much as the gentleman driving it. It was a smart phaeton with room for only two. The passenger was a fashionable lady. The driver was Mr. Wakefield.

Annabelle stared. She might have been fastened to the spot. The phaeton passed by in a blur of gold and yellow—the spinning golden spokes of the wheels and a fluttering of the lady's yellow ostrich plumes and yellow silk scarf.

"Miss?" There was a gentle tug on her sleeve. "Miss? Are you well, Miss?"

Annabelle blinked and then looked at Jane's puzzled face.

Annabelle breathed. "Yes. I am very well. I was thinking of something."

"Is there something we forgot, Miss?"

"No, Jane, I do not think so. We have all of Lady Holden's list."

Annabelle's legs were trembling. She hoped the carriage would hurry. Her stomach seemed full of lead; it was difficult to draw a breath.

"You are terrible pale, Miss."

"I—I am not used to city air."

"The carriage ought not to be so long. Truly it ought not."

"It will come soon."

Annabelle began to feel dizzy, and she began to pray for the carriage. Just as she thought her legs must fail, Jane sang out.

"There 'tis! I shall have William take your packages."

Annabelle was numb on the ride back to Lord Holden's townhouse. But when they arrived at last, Annabelle realized what she must do.

"Jane, please have the packages taken to Lady Holden. I have one more errand, but I must go alone."

Jane protested but mildly, but on reassurance from Annabelle, left her with no further demur. Annabelle gave the driver her last request.

"I would like to go to a good employment agency, one where a young woman of good breeding can seek a position. Do you know of such a place?"

"Aye, Miss."

"Then take me there. Now, please."

Gregory cursed his excellent taste. It seemed his fiancée was damnably clever in the bargain, and she was surprisingly agile when it came to ferreting out information from him. She had somehow learned that his savior was a young woman from a household of modest means and the proprietor of a boarding establishment, which was not in itself harmful information, but she additionally gleaned from something he must have said that this young woman was attractive.

No, he was certain he had not let fall any such word from his lips; but it did not matter. She *knew* his concern for his guardian angel was not objective.

"You must simply reward her in keeping with the service she rendered, and be done with it."

"That is my intention."

"Then why have you mentioned her mortgaged property? I should not think that of relevance at all. It is unfortunate for her, but it is nothing you are responsible for."

Gregory bit his tongue. He should have realized that Miss Abbotsley would seize upon the odd bit of information like a dog upon a fresh bone. He did not recall having this particular problem with her in the past, but it seemed they had not encountered a difference of opinion before. She and he had always been of like mind. There had never been anything else to consider beyond the practical matters of money and status and family, his introducing her cousin in the

House of Lords, what changes might be made at Kilburn, and the like.

Certainly, there had been nothing of a passionate nature.

He turned the phaeton into the entrance of Hyde Park.

"I should hope," she was saying, "that with our being formally engaged and being seen *toujours ensemble* as we are, that you keep our reputations in mind. It would not do at all for any little gallantry of yours to some little nobody from the country to be talked about."

"I shall not be gallant," said Gregory through lightly clenched teeth.

"Also, we do need to set a wedding date. You have disposed of Harry's little problem, and I think we have no worry now on that head."

"No. No worry at all." He wondered what Miss Abbotsley would think if she knew that her fiancé might be a rather larger worry. That very night he planned to rub shoulders with some quite nefarious characters.

"I should like you to come by this evening and share a drink with my father. He has been quite concerned since your misadventure."

"I shall come by, but not tonight. I have an engagement."

Mistake!

"What engagement can you have tonight? It is nothing that I am aware of."

"I should think not. I meet with some gentlemen friends."

"Gentlemen friends?"

"Er—political friends. It is of a business nature."

"I cannot understand this. You have scarcely come

back and have not been to Westminster nor called on anyone."

"Nevertheless, I have an engagement."

"Whom shall you see?"

Gregory, who was pained at telling an untruth, finally uttered the one thing that guaranteed him victory. "I am sorry, my dear, but a gentleman has his duty. Surely you would not question it."

Miss Abbotsley, for all her curiosity and determination to know all, also knew *her* duty. The place of a wife, or a future wife, was to support her husband and not intrude upon her husband's business—particularly anything related to his duty to England. Miss Abbotsley lifted her chin and stared straight ahead, giving no further argument but not exuding waves of pleasure, either.

Gregory breathed deep in relief.

Annabelle hadn't ridden far in the carriage before her practical mind began to take over her emotions. Her entire life had taught her not to act on impulse, and an impulse in such a direction—to advertise for employment—was nevertheless an impulse. For one, she had no letter of reference; she supposed one could be obtained, but it was not a thing that could be done on the instant.

Secondly, her own situation notwithstanding, there were others to think of. There was Mother, who had explicitly and tearfully commanded that she not take a position. Her mother might be impractical, but this did give her pause. She also must consider how her absence would affect Mother and Hartleigh and all who resided there.

She would earn little as a governess, at least in the beginning, and if she did not eventually find a place in a good family, she might never have but a pittance to set aside. She might support herself, but she would be in no position to help the others.

It all came back to Hartleigh. Without scrupulous management, Hartleigh would be lost; and Mother had no means of support without Hartleigh. Whatever solution Annabelle attempted, the future of Hartleigh must figure into it.

She rapped on the carriage roof.

"I have changed my mind," she said to the driver. "Take me back to Hertford Street."

Harry would make a fine spy, Gregory thought. In excellent time, Harry was able to inform Gregory where he might find Ridlington that evening. Ridlington would be playing at a gambling hell called Hargreaves, a place known for deep play and an interesting mix of the notable as well as the notorious among its patrons.

"He usually begins the evening with a couple of turns at roulette, and then he seeks partners in play," Harry had said. "He has a customary table in the back right of the room, and he sits so his back is to the wall and he faces outward, so he can see all who enter and leave. He will play any sort of card game—piquet, vingt-et-un, faro."

Harry also knew the trick of entering this particular hell, which was done by means of a secret knock and a password.

Gregory said nothing about Harry's particular knowledge of gaming and the gaming society. He hoped Harry had learned his lesson, but Harry was no longer a child.

Gregory was ashamed, in fact, to learn that Harry had turned nineteen. Even before being bumped on the head, Gregory had thought of Harry as seventeen, the age Harry had been when Father had passed away. It was time for Gregory to trust his younger brother's experience to be his teacher. And quite clearly, it was also time for Gregory to slow down and appreciate life. But first there was this little matter to settle.

"I still cannot like it," Harry said. "I cannot remember the last time you played."

They had exited their carriage some little walk away from their destination, for the remainder of the route was but an alley too narrow for the carriage to pass. It made for a dangerous walk, but it did maintain anonymity. Neither crests upon expensive equipages nor ostentatious dress were seen here.

Gregory turned down the narrow street with his brother, keeping a watchful eye about him. "Have faith," he said quietly. "By some ironic whim of fate, I was given an excellent mind for cards. There are, of course, no guarantees."

"As one who very recently could not remember his name," Harry said dryly, "I find your confidence— shall I say—a bit remarkable."

"My dear Harry, I am even wiser than before. Among other things, I can now milk a cow." He smiled.

"Good Lord! You are supposed to milk *Ridlington*."

"Precisely. I shall grasp him *so* and squeeze. Stop fretting."

It was dark as the inside of a drum in the alley, with hints of moonlight here and there, mostly outlining the ramshackle row of building tops above them. The various stoops and doorways were mostly deserted, and a pair of scrawny dogs rooted in a pile of refuse. Gregory kept one hand in his coat pocket, cautiously holding the butt of his loaded pistol. With the other hand he carried his heavy-headed cane, which left no hand free to guard his nose from the stench. In time, he knew, he would become inured to it.

They reached the door of the establishment. It was set into the wall, of heavy wood, and otherwise obscure. Harry delivered the requisite knock.

A rough-looking fellow opened the door. "What business have you?" he growled.

"Brother of the Bung," said Harry.

The man grunted and stepped aside. They stepped into a small entrance alcove.

By plan, Harry paused. Gregory walked on to the next doorway and glanced into the card room proper. With one brief perusal he saw several persons he knew among the players, including those he expected. He also saw Ridlington in the back corner, just as Harry had said. Gregory slipped behind a group of gentlemen near the wall and made his way carefully to the back, reasonably assured that Ridlington had not observed him.

Ridlington was having his sport with a green-looking young gentleman who appeared to be realizing the difficulty he was in. The young man's cheeks were flushed pink, and his hair had been considerably mussed by his worried fingers. They were at piquet, and Ridlington was the dealer.

"Game," Ridlington said softly. "I must say, you have had bad luck."

Gregory judged it appropriate then to introduce Ridlington to his own bad luck. Gregory stepped forward.

"Good evening, Ridlington. Still fleecing the innocent, I see."

Ridlington's head jerked around. Even with his

practiced deadpan look, there was no denying his face drained white.

"Swain!"

Gregory paused long enough to see what Ridlington might add, but he said nothing more. Clearly he was struggling with some degree of shock. *Cunning bastard*, Gregory thought. *No, I am not dead.*

"I heard I might find you here," Gregory said.

Ridlington seemed to collect himself. "I should not have expected you to look for me. Certainly not in a place so . . . distasteful to you."

"Ah, but I have given it thought and realized I very much wanted to have a game."

"You?" Ridlington's appearance was now composed, but his voice betrayed a hint of anxiety. "This is indeed a revelation."

"I thought you might feel that way. You see, I have come to the realization that *life is short*, and I had been mistaken in not partaking in all it has to offer. And it occurred to me: Who better to have a game with than Ridlington? So you see, I have come."

Ridlington pinched his lips together. A strange silence had fallen over the room. More faces turned their way, and a small crowd began to gather.

"I should perhaps remind you that your esteemed father did not have luck," Ridlington said.

"Nor did my brother," Gregory added smoothly. "But I plan on being otherwise, and I have been lucky so far, would you not say?" He paused, watching Ridlington's face for the desired effect. Then Gregory smiled.

"I have a stake you cannot refuse, my friend. If you win, you may be guaranteed that I shall not trouble you again. If I win, then I shall have to be a great deal of trouble to you, I fear."

Ridlington grew paler still. "I cannot think what you are talking about."

"And if those stakes are not enough, I shall also place another wager upon the table. I have a very pretty little estate in Kent; I believe you know it. Come—name your counterbet." He paused, and then added, "I happen to know that you hold the note on a property called Hartleigh in Leicestershire. It will do to start."

Ridlington's eyes sharpened. "What is your interest in that? It is of no great value."

"My interest," said Gregory smoothly, "is in having a game. That is all you are required to know."

"You are mad, Swain." Ridlington blinked. "Not that I will protest an easy win."

"Not so easy," Gregory purred. "There is a condition. I must have witnesses."

At his words, four gentlemen stepped forward from the crowd of onlookers. Three were Gregory's friends; the third was Harry.

"This is preposterous!" snapped Ridlington. "An insult!"

Gregory leaned close until his lips were only inches from Ridlington's ear. "Still, much better than a gibbet, would you not say?" he said softly. "I suggest you play."

Chapter Thirteen

Gregory did not know if he could win against Ridlington. Ridlington was a very cunning player, even when he had no opportunity to cheat and quite possibly even under considerable stress. Of himself, Gregory did know that he possessed more than sufficient skill to defeat most men. He was adept at reading faces, was a masterful strategist, and had a memory for detail that was the envy of most men he knew. Whatever the outcome, Ridlington would not find an easy win.

The warm-up time Gregory required was sufficient to reassure Ridlington at first. Finding his footing, Gregory took care not to reveal his ability too soon, but by the time they had completed two hands, his secret was out. Ridlington knew he had a worthy opponent.

The room remained in studious silence as the circle of observers concentrated on the game. The score was close, and Gregory would have been more concerned had he not observed the beads of sweat on Ridlington's upper lip.

Gregory would miss the little estate in Kent if he were to lose, he thought. It would have been home to one of his children, or perhaps a wedding gift to Harry. But more than this he would regret not winning Hartleigh for Miss Dearborn.

The clock ticked on. They were now in the last, deciding hand. Gregory focused. The deal had been completed, and the declaring began.

"Four."

"How much?"

"Thirty-seven."

"Good."

"Tierce."

"How high?"

"King."

"Not good. Ace."

"Sequence of four."

"Good."

Declarations ended and the play started. Gregory led the first card, watching his opponent carefully. Ridlington played, won the trick, and led back. Gregory played and lost again. Ridlington led out once more.

"Palming," Gregory said softly.

"What are you talking about?" Ridlington sputtered.

"I request that your hand be counted. You should not have been holding the ace of spades. I suspect you made an 'unofficial draw.'"

"And discard," said Harry. "A deuce is under his chair."

"May we examine your coat?" Gregory asked mildly.

"The devil you will!" Ridlington jumped up. "A card was dropped! We have a new deal, that is all!"

Gregory blinked disarmingly. "New deal, then. But first, take off your coat, and push up your sleeves."

The audience began to mutter. Gregory held up his hand.

"Please, gentlemen. I shall take off my coat as well, and we shall go on. Silence, if you will."

Ridlington sat, and the last hand began again. The room was still but for the sound of Gregory's and Ridlington's voices as they declared, Gregory's calm, Ridlington's terse.

The play began. One trick after another was taken, until the final one remained. That trick went to Gregory.

Gregory leaned back. "One fifty-seven," he said softly. "I believe you are at one seventeen. That gives me one forty for game. I win, Ridlington."

Ridlington stared. Then, slowly, he rose.

"You may have Hartleigh," he snarled, "and welcome."

"Thank you. My companions will accompany you and secure the note—and my cash winnings as well."

Ridlington cursed.

"As for you, my friend, I offer this bit of advice: take what you have remaining to you and leave England. That is so much neater than a trial."

Harry walked with Gregory to his carriage, displaying his youthful high spirits. "I cannot believe how splendid you were!" Harry laughed. "You old slyboots, keeping your talent under your hat! That's famous; that's what that is!"

"Yes, I suppose, but remember the most important part of the lesson: that I never play—save this once, when I almost lost."

"Oh, be done with moralizing, will you, Gory? I should like one moment of celebration, at the very least."

Gregory smiled slightly. It had been a very long

time since he'd heard Harry's childhood name for him. "Very well, then. Just this one moment."

They reached the main street, and Gregory withdrew his hand from his pistol pocket and rubbed his brow. His headache seemed to be back.

"I should think you would be a bit happy yourself," Harry said.

They paused at the gas lamp to await the carriage.

"Life is full of oddities," Gregory said. "You believe I should be happy. I, however, only count myself as grateful that I can now make a lasting gift to the woman I love."

Harry hesitated, apparently dumbstruck. Another group of men emerged from the alley, talking and laughing. It was Ridlington's escort, and Harry intended to accompany them. But Harry made no move toward leaving.

"You love Miss Abbotsley?" Harry asked incredulously.

Gregory, who was staring blankly into the street, turned and looked at Harry, his eyes grave and censorious. Harry stared back. Then, Gregory exploded with laughter.

He laughed so hard he doubled over, and Harry's peals of hilarity blended in with his.

Gregory straightened up, gasping.

"I take it I was incorrect!" Harry said in another spurt of laughter.

Gregory composed himself. "Do not expect me to make such an ungentlemanly admission! Now, you had better go, or miss your excitement."

Harry blinked, sobering nearly as quickly as Gregory had. "I can miss it. I should like to know with whom you are in love." He paused. "If you do not tell me, I shall guess."

Gregory sighed. "Yes, I may as well tell you. It makes not a spit's worth of difference. Her name is Annabelle Dearborn. She is young, beautiful, and the bravest and most generous woman I have ever met."

"I see. The innkeeper."

"It is not precisely an inn. A good family fallen upon hard times opened their doors to save the property. The father is dead. The young woman runs it with help from the servants. Her mother lives there as well but does not take part in the business matters."

"And the property is Hartleigh?"

"Of course. I am sure you cannot think of another reason I should be interested in winning an obscure property in Leicestershire. Ridlington had tricked her father into signing possession of it over to him. He has been collecting exorbitant payments from her and her mother since her father died."

Harry whistled. "And so you have saved them. You are an out-and-out Robin Hood, Gory."

"As I said, it is the only thing I can give." He looked then into his younger brother's eyes. "You must give me your word that you will not expose me. Miss Abbotsley would be unhappy in the extreme, and the gossip would be atrocious. I can withstand it, but I doubt Miss Abbotsley will wish to."

Harry cleared his throat. "Don't worry about me," he said. "I shall be faithful until the end."

"Good. Townsend, Abbot and Kingsley will not speak of it, I know, but of course they do not know the particulars about Miss Dearborn. They only know that I should not like the gambling tale to be made public."

Harry cracked a little smile. "I wonder if the *ton* would believe it? I can, hardly. Dash it all, you aren't the same brother. That knock on the head ruined your starch and propriety completely."

Gregory raised his brows. "Not completely. I think I have learned there are exceptions to every rule. I did tend to be a little . . . rigid in the past."

"Rigid!" Harry chuckled. "You were fossilized! You terrified everyone but Mother and Miss Abbotsley! But, of course, Miss Abbotsley is even more frightening than you were."

Gregory cleared his throat. "You are speaking of a lady."

Harry, having found him out, showed no fear. His eyes twinkled merrily. "My deepest apologies, old fellow. Shouldn't have said that." He paused. "But it's true!"

The carriage came rolling up to the curb with a clatter of hooves and wheel against stone.

"Shall you return with me, then?" Gregory asked.

"I would, but I believe I may still catch the others. I should like to help Ridlington part with your winnings. I shall see you tomorrow, Gory!"

Gregory watched Harry hurry away, waving and shouting at the men entering the carriage just down the street.

"Good-bye, *Horrible Harry*," he said softly, watching his baby brother cross into manhood. And then he boarded his own carriage and headed for home.

The morning following her unhappy sighting of Wakefield, Annabelle awoke with new resolution. She knew her object now, and regardless of her opinion of it, it had to be achieved. Annabelle must find a husband with the means to preserve Hartleigh.

She arose and readied herself for the day, and at last had Jane assist her into a pretty, yellow figured muslin gown. She had her hair put up with more than her usual care and donned her string of amber beads. Gazing at the result in the looking glass, she wished her face had more color, but she could not fault her toilette.

It was her aunt's at-home day, and there would be visitors. Annabelle intended to be as pretty, as interesting and as charming as possible, and to do what her mother had urged her to do forever: cast about for possible gentlemen.

She did not expect to enjoy the process nor the result. In her situation the best she could hope for would perhaps be an older suitor seeking a second wife, a gentleman who had no particular need to marry for station or money. But if this could save herself and her mother from penury, then this was what she would do.

She left her room with this determination and started to descend the stairs to the breakfast room, and was surprised to meet Aunt Holden coming up. It was not the sight of her aunt in itself that surprised her, but rather that she appeared to be examining a letter in her hand, and the moment Annabelle greeted her, Aunt Holden quickly thrust the letter behind her skirts.

"Oh, how you startled me!" said her aunt.

Annabelle paused. "I am coming down for breakfast. I did not know you rose early as well," Annabelle said. "Mother will not be up for hours yet."

"I know." Aunt Holden smiled slightly. "I do enjoy a little solitude early in the morning. I always have. Do you have plans for the day?"

"I intend to be here for callers." Annabelle smiled back at her aunt. "I see you have received a note already. Is it an invitation?"

Aunt Holden's smile faltered, and she looked absolutely caught out. Aunt Holden's face, her mother had always said, was "absolutely transparent."

"An invitation? Ah, no, I do not think so. Or, perhaps it is. I do not know. I have not looked at it yet."

Aunt Holden looked very much as if she wished to escape, but Annabelle did not mean to let her. "How very mysterious you are! Look at it now. I should like a little diversion."

Thus cornered, Aunt Holden finally brought forth the letter from her skirts. "It is—oh, dear me. It is not addressed to me at all. It is addressed to you."

"Oh, really?" Annabelle held out her hand, hiding her astonishment behind her smile. But Aunt Holden did not relinquish the letter immediately.

"Annabelle—" She paused, flustered. "Oh, dear. I— I am not certain how to say this, but I do not wish you to leave."

Annabelle stared at her, bewildered. "Leave? Why would we leave?" Her eyes fell to the letter, and she caught a glimpse of the handwriting. It was regular and strong, and a sudden suspicion hit her.

"It is from Wakefield," she said. She looked up at her aunt's guilty face.

"Yes, I fear it is. You see, I—I am afraid you and my sister will leave as soon as you have means to travel. I know what you think of me, but it is not true. I want to help you both. But Lord Holden—"

"I understand, Aunt Holden," Annabelle said gently. "I believe Mother does, as well. May I have the letter, please?"

Reluctantly, Aunt Holden passed it over to her.

"I have been so worried," Annabelle said, eagerly breaking the seal. Her hands were trembling, and she hoped Aunt did not notice. She glanced up at her aunt again. "Aunt Holden, has Wakefield written before this?"

Aunt Holden looked positively mournful. "Yes, he has. Only to say he was safe and would be in touch." She paused, clutching her hands together nervously. "I am sorry I did not give it to you. I meant it for the best."

Annabelle busied herself with opening the missive while she sorted through her emotions. Wakefield had written—and Aunt Holden had intercepted the note! It was a horrid thing for her to have done. But on the other hand, she had not meant harm, only good. Aunt Holden had been trying to keep them in London.

Annabelle opened the folded paper. It was two notes she saw, with a second note folded inside the first. And the first note—

Annabelle gave a soft gasp and then slowly sank down to sit upon the stair.

"Goodness, what is it?" cried Aunt Holden.

It was a moment before Annabelle could answer. She looked up at last, hardly able to believe what she held in her hand.

"It is the promissory note for Hartleigh," she said.

Aunt Holden looked bewildered. "What does that mean? I thought you no longer possessed Hartleigh."

Annabelle assessed her aunt's countenance and realized that she did not understand such things as promissory notes. Aunt would be satisfied that her husband did and be content.

"Father's debts were not completely paid when he passed away. There was still this loan he had taken out on Hartleigh. It has been such a struggle to pay, and now it is gone! We owned Hartleigh in name only, and now we have it back in all respects. Hartleigh is ours completely."

"Oh."

Annabelle picked up the smaller note. She opened it.

Dear Miss Dearborn,

I realize this is a surprise to you, but I hope it is a happy one. I have been able to obtain the enclosed note on Hartleigh, and I hereby return it to you. It is given as a token of my gratitude for the service you have rendered to me, which can never be fully repaid.

I must ask, however, that you do not inquire about the details of this matter. Suffice it to say that Hartleigh is now legally, rightfully, and truly yours.

For the rest, I must regretfully tell you that our ways must part from this time. It is not by my desire but rather by necessity that I say this. I sincerely wish you all the best of happiness, health, and good fortune, all the most pure and precious of blessings, throughout a very long and rewarding life. I can only regret being unable to share it with you.

Remember me with fondness.

I am,

J. Wakefield.

Annabelle read the letter over three times and stared at it until the writing swam before her eyes.

"Annabelle?" came her aunt's worried voice.

Annabelle took a breath and looked up at her aunt, who stood clutching the stair rail and looking as though a touch could tumble her down.

"I am well," Annabelle said. She paused to bite her lip, which was starting to tremble. "Wakefield is leaving us. That is all. I—"

Her voice began to fail. Turning her face, she rose to her feet. "I must go and tell Mother." Then she turned and rapidly retraced her steps up the stairs.

Chapter Fourteen

Mother was overjoyed, as Annabelle believed she would be. "We own Hartleigh again!" she exclaimed. "It is the most wonderful news I have had since you became engaged to—oh, never mind that. We are saved, my poppet!"

Annabelle sat quietly on the edge of the chaise in Mother's room. Mother, who had been lying back on the chaise when Annabelle entered, now sat bolt upright, waving the note about in unbridled enthusiasm.

Mother had stopped herself from mentioning Mr. Harwell. Annabelle could forgive her, even if she recalled him all the same.

"It is not all repaired," Annabelle said. "We have very little money. But at least we do not have to pay Lord Ridlington any longer."

"Well, I am very pleased with that," Mother said in an admonishing tone. "As for the rest, all we need now is for you to make a good match. You are yet young enough, and the property is worth something. We must be about the business as soon as possible! Stand up, dear. I wish to turn about."

Annabelle stood, and her mother neatly turned on the chaise and placed her slippered feet upon the floor. She did not stand, however, but continued to speak. Annabelle sat in the nearby wing chair.

"I have to wonder how Mr. Wakefield managed to obtain this note," Mother went on. "He must have remembered who he is, and he is rich! There is no other explanation."

"He does not say, Mother."

"One only reads between the lines. He said that we must part ways, which can only mean he is someone of very high rank. I wish I could determine who he is. I shall have to ask your aunt if she has heard of any mysterious disappearances. It must be known. And his return would be talked of all over London!"

"And if it is not?"

"Then he is a commoner, but he still must be rich . . . and likely married." Mother paused then, a small frown furrowing her brow. "How horrid it is. I think he would marry you if he could. His letter expressed his affection very clearly."

Annabelle lowered her gaze to her aunt's red and gold Turkish rug, fixing on the place where a golden column of morning light made its brilliant colors bloom and glimmer.

"He is grateful to us, Mother. I do not think we should make more of it than that."

"My dear, however did you become so spiritless? You did not acquire it from me! To have something of value one must fight for it. It is the same with women as it is with men—except more difficult."

Annabelle bit her tongue. Had she not been fighting all these months to save Hartleigh, performing a man's office and a man's work while Mother closed herself away in despair? But she had to acknowledge that Mother had a valid point. Mother had found her strength again, and Annabelle had lost hers.

She could only think of losing Mr. Wakefield . . . and wonder how in the world she would ever repay him for Hartleigh.

Two days after the receipt of the note from Wakefield, an invitation came. The butler delivered it to Aunt Holden's hand as the ladies sat in the morning room.

Aunt Holden and Mrs. Dearborn were discussing the mystery of Mr. Wakefield again; Aunt Holden knew of no gentleman of high rank who had recently vanished and reappeared, so the puzzle was an engrossing one. The arrival of the invitation put a pause to the discussion, and Annabelle and her mother sat quietly at their needlework while Aunt Holden opened the invitation.

Aunt Holden scanned the writing and burst into animated speech.

"Oh, my dears! Only guess! My dear friend Lady Locksley has included you in her invitation for Thursday! Oh, I so hoped for this!"

"Is it true?" Mother exclaimed. "Let me see the invitation!"

The precious piece of paper was passed into Mother's hand. All the while Aunt kept up her stream of ecstatic words.

"We are all to attend her fête champêtre together! I have done it! You are to be received back into society! I can hardly speak! I am trembling!"

"Sister—oh, dear, but I have so longed for this! I can hardly believe—"

The sisters leapt to their feet together and fell into each other's arms, both weeping, while Annabelle watched, a tear slipping down her own face. Such happiness in her mother she had never expected to see again.

Only Annabelle knew how truly a momentous event the invitation was, for Lady Locksley was the person who had advised her to withdraw from her engagement to Mr. Harwell. Such, Annabelle thought, was the change an increase in fortune brought. The recovery of Hartleigh was to reintroduce them to the worthy and capricious *ton*.

The intervening days passed rapidly. As Annabelle and her mother were late additions to Lord and Lady Holden's invitation, there was little time for them to prepare. Still, in her rose silk gown, an ivory shawl trimmed with blond lace and her amber beads, Annabelle realized she looked as well as she possibly could. It was a good thing, for this event was in all likelihood the most elegant she would attend during her stay in London. The fête champêtre was to take place at Lady Locksley's elegant home on the edge of the city, and it was to be one of the most notable events of the season.

There was a half-moon and a coolish breeze the evening they set their carriage for the Locksley estate. Annabelle could not help but feel anticipation, in spite of the ever-present ache in the area of her heart. Her plans had not changed. If anything, the return of the note on Hartleigh with Wakefield's farewell enclosed had set her mind. If she could not increase her happiness, she could increase her assets. The specter of poverty was yet too close for comfort.

They were forced to wait for some time in a long string of carriages on the approach to Locksley Hall. They advanced at a crawl, and Annabelle's anxiety turned to restlessness. Mother remained quiet, and it seemed her mind was elsewhere. Aunt Holden seemed to be deep in her own thoughts as well, and neither appeared to notice when someone in the carriage ahead of them emptied out the window a can that had apparently been used for the necessary, a thing that Annabelle found vulgar in the extreme.

Then again, Annabelle had spent most of her life in the country, while Mother and Aunt Holden were accustomed to London's ways. Perhaps this odd behavior meant nothing to them. In any event, the long wait did nothing to improve Annabelle's spirits, and when their carriage did at last roll to the door, she felt she had escaped from prison.

Annabelle had had one previous occasion to visit the Locksley home, and that had been four years ago when she had been an impressionable eighteen. Still, with its gay adornment for the evening, it seemed every bit as splendid tonight as it had the first time.

The circular drive in front of the stately home was lined with glowing lanterns, and the front portico was overhung with garlands of roses. In the exquisite crush they were let into the great hall, and crowded around them were the most au courant of ladies and gentlemen.

Annabelle was encompassed by the scents of perfume and hot wax and perspiration, and the heat from so many dozens of close bodies enveloped her like a blanket. Candlelight glowed on jewel-colored silks and satins as if a stained-glass window had splintered and lent its colors to the gowns. There was conversation punctuated by the occasional laugh or exclamation, and by the distant strains of a quartet.

From their reception in the great hall, the flow of guests pressed on through the ballroom and then out onto the large back terrace, and Annabelle with her mother, her aunt, and Lord Holden was pushed along with it. At last, on the terrace, the crowd diminished as the guests found their way down the terrace steps into the garden, where refreshment tables were set up beneath gaily colored tents adorned with more roses and boughs of greenery.

Here Annabelle paused to drink in the view. Below, beyond the classically columned terrace, lay the most festive and extravagant sight she had ever seen.

Outlining the flower-draped tents and stationed as far as she could see along the garden paths were the hanging lanterns, glowing golden like giant fireflies and illuminating the nearby trees. In the center of the garden under another canopy was a raised dais, and from here the quartet sent sweet strains floating into the night. There was another area covered with a canopy for dancing, and some couples were already waltzing in the light of the lanterns and the blushing moon.

Annabelle looked about her for her mother and saw her a little distance away in conversation with her aunt and another lady she did not know. Lord Holden had vanished from sight, so for the moment she was alone.

She was thankful for that. For now she wanted to be an observer, to see all and commit it to memory. She felt strongly that she did not belong here in this assembly of glitter and wealth, but she could very well enjoy the spectacle.

Oh, but how much more would she rather be home at Hartleigh, spending ordinary hours in Mr. Wakefield's company!

"Here is my daughter," came her mother's voice. "Annabelle dear, come and be introduced to these ladies."

Annabelle pasted a smile on her face and turned to

her mother. There were two ladies with her besides
Aunt Holden, and she recognized neither of them.

"Lady Hanson, Lady Crowell, my daughter Miss
Dearborn."

Annabelle accepted their limp hands in turn, ex-
pressing her pleasure in their acquaintance.

"You are very lovely, dear," said Lady Hanson.

"Yes, is she not?" replied Lady Crowell. "I can quite
see how a gentleman's head might be turned."

"Congratulations on your *good fortune*, Miss Dearborn."

There was something in the tone of the ladies'
voices that did not sound like mere pleasantry, but
rather had a disturbing archness about it. When they
stepped away, Annabelle looked at her mother and
aunt questioningly. Her aunt made the barest ac-
knowledgement of her question with a puzzled lift of
her eyebrows. Mother was more forthcoming.

"No one should know about Hartleigh unless they
were told by someone. I cannot think it was one of
us." Mother's voice sounded faintly accusatory.

"Oh, no! Not one of us!" said Aunt Holden. "Absolutely not! I did mention it to Lady Locksley, of
course, but she is a very good friend and the soul of
discretion. When she is asked to keep a confidence,
she always does. *Nothing* can prize a thing from her
lips once she is determined to keep silent on it. I *did*
need to mention it, you know, to get an invitation for
you and Annabelle. I felt certain she would then ex-
tend you hospitality, and she has."

"I realize that, and I do appreciate it, Caroline," said
Mother. "But clearly something is being said by some-
one."

Annabelle sighed. "I should not say this, but really,
I am past caring. What difference can it make? We

needed some pretense to fortune to be invited, and yet we cannot have it talked of. I am all at sixes and sevens."

"It is the method of our recovery that is best not discussed," her mother said. "A gift such as we received would certainly be questioned. Well, what is done is done; we shall see what we shall see."

Mother and Aunt said nothing more on the subject, and presently Annabelle realized they were looking about with discriminating eyes.

"Mr. Simon," said Aunt Holden. "He has been widowed above a year, and he is here, over near the fountain with that young woman in green. He has adequate income and is respectable enough. What do you think of him?"

Annabelle looked when her mother did. Mr. Simon was perhaps in his fifties and slightly portly, and Annabelle could tell nothing else about him from their distance.

"Possibly," Mother said. "But I see Mr. Henley over by the refreshments. He is younger. I believe his wife died shortly before my John did. Is he yet unmarried, Caroline?"

"Yes, I do believe he is."

Annabelle looked at Mr. Henley. He was indeed younger and possessed, in Annabelle's opinion, a fish face.

"Ah. Do you remember Mr. Carter, Eleanor? He is here!" Aunt Holden pointed. "He did not used to have a feather to fly with! His situation must have changed."

Mother looked, and so did Annabelle. Annabelle saw a solidly formed man with broad shoulders and silver-gray hair tied back in an old-fashioned queue.

He was in his dress regimentals and had an air of stateliness about him.

"But he is a captain now, Caroline! Only look at his uniform."

"Oh, yes! How silly of me."

"Annabelle," Mother said softly. "Captain Carter is an extremely agreeable gentleman. If his fortune has changed . . ."

Mother and Aunt were trying to find her a husband, and Annabelle felt nothing. Nevertheless, it was a necessary business—and Captain Carter was the first interesting prospect, despite his age. She guessed he was Mother's age or a bit older, solidly in his forties.

"I find nothing the matter with his looks, save he is old."

" 'Old,' " snapped Mother, "is not an objection for your situation. I am acquainted with Captain Carter, and if he is acceptable on all other counts, you could not do better."

Annabelle sighed inwardly. No, she likely could *not* do better. It was such a pity she must marry at all. But if she were not in love, perhaps she could bear the inevitable disappointment that attached itself to gentlemen.

"Come, let us introduce him," said Mother.

Annabelle followed Mother and Aunt Holden down the terrace steps and through the colorful throng. As they approached the gentleman, Annabelle noticed how tall he was, and when he turned toward them, she saw he had a roughly hewn face that had seen many campaigns.

"Captain Carter. It is very good to see you after so long," Mother said. She smiled dazzlingly and extended a hand.

For the briefest moment Captain Carter gazed at Mother as if bemused, then pleasure shone in his eyes.

"Miss—er, Mrs. Dearborn! It has indeed been long! I should say many years, but you do not look as though you have lived above half of them." He took Mother's gloved hand and kissed it gently.

Mother seemed to blush. It was hard to tell in the dim light.

"You flatter me. But I have a grown daughter here with me, my only child, Miss Dearborn. Annabelle, meet Captain Carter."

He had kind eyes, Annabelle saw. She wondered how he and Mother had known each other.

"You are lovely, just like your mother," he said, and kissed her hand as well.

"Pleased to meet you, Captain Carter. Thank you for your kind words, but I must disagree with you. Mother is by far lovelier."

He smiled. "I cannot reply without finding myself in difficulties, I see," he said. "Mrs. Dearborn, are things well with you?"

"They are as they are. My husband passed away, you may have heard. We have been staying in the country but decided to come to visit my sister and her husband."

"I am very sorry about your husband."

"Oh, but one deals as one must. And how may you be?"

"Lonely, I must say. I have been a widower for many years and found it expedient not to marry again, but at this time in my career—well, I have retired. And so I am visiting with *my* sister in London as well. I did not dream I should meet you here."

"Is that not remarkable that we are both visiting sisters! And how odd we should meet here in this crowded place!"

"Not odd. A miracle. I believe it is magic at work. Do you not feel it?"

This time Annabelle knew Mother blushed. At that moment she knew that she needed to leave them to their own conversation.

Annabelle distanced herself by several paces and stopped near Aunt Holden, who had fallen into conversation with a passing friend who thankfully was not asking questions about the Dearborns' return to fortune. For a few moments Annabelle wondered about Mother's old acquaintance with Captain Carter and what their obvious pleasure in meeting again could mean. Her reverie was interrupted by the rising murmurs around her.

She glanced about and realized that many were directing their attention toward the terrace. Consequently, she looked there; and then, her world stopped.

At the top of the terrace steps stood a very fine couple—an elegant lady in silver-spangled sky blue and a handsome gentleman in black.

Dear God. Mr. Wakefield.

"Oh, no, dear. That is Lord Swain!" Aunt Holden answered.

Annabelle realized with a start that she had spoken aloud.

"If you were in London for a time," her aunt continued, "you would not make that mistake! He is an earl of a long and distinguished line. I believe that is his fiancée with him. How in the *world* can you mistake him for your coachman?"

Annabelle felt she was dying a thousand deaths. Each breath she took pained her to the center of her being and felt quite as though it must be her last; but still she must take another, and another.

Lord Swain. An earl. No wonder he had sent such a gift and severed their relationship! Such a man would be no stranger to such a thing. He would know just how to make such a parting, and it was likely the cost of the note on Hartleigh was small to him.

Aunt Holden, who was slow to understand but not entirely obtuse, abruptly declared, "But Lord Swain has not been missing! I should have heard if he had been!"

Annabelle ignored her aunt's outburst and stepped close to her mother once more, who was now staring at Lord Swain much as Annabelle had done. "Mother," Annabelle whispered, "I must leave."

Annabelle's mother lowered her lips near Annabelle's ear. "Absolutely not," she said with icy firmness. "When the opportunity presents itself, which it may, you will greet him in an ordinary manner. You will under no circumstances mention the gift, but you will be gracious. He is a most valuable friend to have."

A valuable friend! Annabelle wished she could vanish into the ground. *Mr. Wakefield* had been a friend. She knew not what Lord Swain was to her, but likely he did not expect to see her here.

A short while passed. Mother made small talk with Captain Carter and Aunt Holden. Annabelle, in an agony of nerves, kept clandestine watch of Lord Swain and his fiancée, praying that they came no closer and made a quick departure. As she spied upon Lord Swain, however, it became more and more evident to Annabelle that she and her mother were being watched as well. More than once she caught the guarded glance of a lady, who quickly looked away and consequently had something to say to her companion behind her fan.

Annabelle by turns looked to her mother to see how she fared, then cautiously about her again. She could not determine if Lord Swain had noticed her or not. Could he know that he and she were possibly the subjects of an *on-dit*? What would be the result if they were to meet in front of so many eyes? Perhaps it would not matter. Likely he was prudent enough not to convey recognition of her. That would, of course, make her humiliation complete.

Annabelle leaned close to her mother's ear. "I must go to the ladies' withdrawing room, Mother."

"Just a moment, my dear—"

"I shall return."

Annabelle stepped rapidly away, threading quickly between the clots of guests, knowing that she had left her party astonished at her behavior. It did not matter. She had to escape, to secret herself alone for at least a short while, and compose her emotions and her thoughts. The withdrawing room was the best destination she could conceive of. However, she quickly realized that she could not go *there* without passing dangerously close to Lord Swain and his fiancée on her way to the terrace steps.

There was no time to think of a better plan. Turning back, she headed instead toward the back of the extensive garden, slipping quickly down a shadowed path and turning down its darkest ways. In a few moments, the lanterns ceased to light the way, and her guide became the silvery pattern of moonlight.

She turned one corner and found herself confronting a couple indulging in an amorous kiss. Quickly circumventing them, she went on. At last she came to the wooded verge of the garden and spotted a small cottage just a little farther on. Holding her silk skirts close to avoid the brush and brambles, she quietly approached and found it to be not a cottage, but a small pavilion overgrown with ivy.

Annabelle climbed the shallow wooden steps carefully, and they bowed beneath her weight. Reaching the top, she peered through the open archway within.

It was very old. In the slivers of moonlight shining through the ivied lattice, there was nothing to see but scattered dead leaves, twigs and cobwebs. There were no lovers present at least, unless of the rodent variety, but Annabelle did not fear that.

There was a circular bench ringing the inside perimeter of the pavilion. Batting away the cobwebs in her path, she made her way inside and sank down upon the bench to think.

What could she do? Even if she were to escape meeting with Lord Swain tonight, the gossip would follow her. Lord Swain would be embarrassed, and she . . . she would never be able to make a match now that she was the subject of scandal again.

A shadow fell across the entrance.

Annabelle sat paralyzed as the steps creaked and the shadow grew taller before her eyes. It formed the proportions of a large man.

"Miss Dearborn?" It was a soft, familiar voice—a voice that made her heart leap and her stomach harden into a knot.

"Miss Dearborn, it is only I."

Lord Swain paused for a brief moment. She did not respond. The drumming of her heart was beating all sense from her head.

"I saw you," he continued quietly. "I wished to speak with you, but it did not seem possible. Then I saw you leaving. I found an excuse to follow."

Annabelle steeled herself. She did not know why he had followed her, but she foresaw that no good would come of it. She found the breath to speak.

"How gallant of you," she said. She had meant to sound cool; but her voice came out something over a whisper.

He stepped up onto the floor, and a board gave a loud squeak.

"Egad. This is a ruin! What are you doing here?"

She sucked in another breath. "I could not find the withdrawing room," she said stiffly.

"One might ask for directions."

"Yes. One might."

He let his breath out wearily. "Miss Dearborn, I came to apologize."

She turned her head toward him, knowing her face was in shadow; the moonlight only touched upon her toes and the hem of her skirt. Of him, she could see nothing but his dark shape.

He took another step, and another creak sounded.

"So long as I do not break a leg in this place."

"Pray do not. I should have to summon help, and I do not believe your fiancée would wish you discovered here with your leg caught in rotted floorboards."

"I am sorry for what has happened. Your welfare—your happiness—is important to me."

The tears came suddenly. She sniffed as silently as she could. "I am sure. That is why, I suppose, you could not as much as tell me your name once you discovered it."

"I wanted to make things easier for you."

Annabelle felt resentment clawing at her throat.

"Easier! Do you suppose a valuable gift from a nameless man makes matters *easier*?"

"Lower your voice," he whispered.

"Even your doxy knows your name! But I am paid off in the same style, without even the benefit of knowing who has done it!"

"Miss Dearborn—" he said sharply, and stopped himself. She could tell he was searching for his self-command.

"Miss Dearborn," he said again more quietly, "*please* speak softly." He paused. "This is quite a different case, and in any event, I do not have doxies!"

"Oh? It seems that others have a different thought on the matter. I find that I am being ogled tonight like a prize calf, to see if I might have met your requirements!"

There was a moment of silence.

"I know nothing of this," he said.

"You have only just arrived." She dabbed her nose. "Apparently your gift of Hartleigh has become the topic of conversation."

He swore softly beneath his breath.

"Have you always been this heedless?" she asked. "I can hardly believe that you followed me."

He sighed. "No. I never was before. This is the first time I have ever been reckless. I feel it is a result of being struck on the head."

"There is an enlightening thought."

"Dash it all, it is because of *you*. I should never have pursued you here for any other reason!"

She struggled to tamp down a sob. "Now it is *my* fault that I am likely to be ruined! I cannot thank you."

"If you will only endeavor to be *quiet*—" He stopped himself. "I am sorry. I am very sorry for the whole of it. It is entirely my fault, and you are quite right."

She swallowed. "You should know that I intend to

pay you for the note on Hartleigh. I shall not be beholden to you in such a way."

"You cannot do that."

"I can, and I shall."

"No, I mean you *cannot* do it. There is no value to repay." He paused. "I won it on a wager."

She gasped softly. "You *won* it?"

"Yes." He shifted his stance, and the boards creaked again. "It seemed the only way to obtain it. I could not buy it from Ridlington, or he should have realized it had some value to me. If he chose to accommodate me, he would have raised the price—as well as questions that I could not answer. Blackmail is not beyond him should he happen upon interesting information." He sighed heavily and, after a brief pause, went on. "Then again, Ridlington being Ridlington, he may have refused to sell."

"Then I should have had to continue paying Ridlington instead of paying you."

"*Secondly,* I anticipated you might insist on repaying me. Since I have won the note, there is no price."

She was silent then, searching for words.

"You are angry because I gambled. I never do. I shall not again. I abhor it."

She drew a tremulous breath. "I have never met such an odd assortment of contradictions as you are."

"And I," he said softly, "can say the same for you."

She was uncertain of his meaning. His tone of voice suggested a caress, and yet his words in themselves were not tender. Her heart clung to his voice, though, wanting to believe it spoke of love . . . foolish though that was, and as ridiculous as *she* was.

The boards creaked again. He had come closer. "Miss Dearborn . . . is there anything I can do so that you do not remember me with contempt?"

Her eyes filled. Here in the dark he could not know, but as she clutched her wadded handkerchief and sought self-control, she knew he would know her secret if she attempted to speak.

"I inherited a fortune from my great uncle," he said, "and my father hated me for it. Father was a drunkard and addicted to gaming, and the family was in ruin. I took control of the family estate from him."

He paused. The boards creaked again.

"I swore I would never gamble. I did it *only* for you."

Her voice, her damnable voice! She could not use it. With every word, he robbed her of more control.

He took another step. "I would do anything in my power for you. I want you to know this. I have never known a woman stronger, more generous, more compassionate than you—or to whom I owe so much."

She gulped. From somewhere she drew strength from sheer force of will.

"You—you are mistaken. I am not so . . . not so—"

He closed the gap between them. There was no more moonlight, only his enveloping shadow, and he reached down and took her arms, drawing her up.

"You must not say—" she began.

"Hush."

"—any more."

That was when his arms slipped around her shoulders, and his soft lips brushed her hair.

"Annabelle . . ."

He kissed her hair. He brushed a soft feathery kiss upon her brow. And then he pulled her tightly to him and pressed her face close.

"Annabelle, how can I let you go?" he whispered.

With her face nestled near the pulse beat in his throat, with her heart so confused, with her being so much in love and so much in pain, she had no words.

He drew a ragged breath.

"Remember me well. Please. This is all I ask."

He let her go.

Suddenly standing alone, her arms empty, she was more devastated than ever before. The cool night breeze wrapped around her where he had been.

She heard him sigh. Then, "Wait a bit after I go; then go back to your mother." He paused. "I shall not forget you."

There were three solid steps, three painful creaks of the old wood floor, then the sound of rapid steps descending the small stair.

He was gone.

Annabelle made her way back to the fete, thankful that the dim lanterns hid the traces of her tears. When she found her mother and aunt at last, Captain Carter was gone. But Lord Holden was there, and he was in a rare temper.

"Where have you been?" he snapped. He leaned close to her and lowered his voice to a taut murmur. "Have you not heard what is being said? Are you seeking to ruin me completely?"

He did not want an answer. He turned away abruptly.

"*Now*, let us go. The carriage is waiting!"

Aunt Holden looked like a frightened little mouse. Mother's face had an expressionless, lifeless look that she wore when she was very troubled and vulnerable.

Annabelle knew her rise in circumstance had ended.

Chapter Fifteen

*L*ord Holden agreed to supply a carriage to transport Annabelle and her mother home to Hartleigh—which *he* preferred to be as soon as possible. Even Mrs. Dearborn agreed confidentially with Annabelle that it was time to leave.

Annabelle, heartsick yet resolved, busied herself the next morning packing her things with Jane's assistance. She no longer cared for London; it was a relief to leave, as much as it spelled an end to any hopes of marriage. She no longer had the strength to battle her emotions. Some way she would deal with their problems when she was back at Hartleigh.

She was very surprised when she was summoned downstairs. She had a visitor.

Tremulous with anxiety, she rushed to ready herself, commanding Jane to help her out of her gown and replace it with the figured white muslin. She could think of no one who would call on her save Lord Swain, and she hardly believed it possible. No, it was impossible, especially after last night, with discovery to be avoided at all cost.

Still, when she presented herself in the morning room minutes later to find it occupied by Mother—

and Miss Abbotsley—her heart fell to the soles of her shoes.

Annabelle sank into a chair, and her mother had only the time to send Annabelle a warning look when Miss Abbotsley began.

"I shall not stay long," she said. "Perhaps you have guessed why I have come. I am the fiancée of Lord Swain. We have been engaged for these two years and more. Therefore, his business is also mine."

Mother spoke. "Indeed, we do not know why you honor us with a visit, Miss Abbotsley."

Miss Abbotsley's chin rose slightly. "Then let me explain. It has come to my ears that there are some rather distressing rumors regarding my fiancée and you, or your daughter, or both." She turned her hard hazel eyes on Annabelle. "I am come to the conclusion that they most certainly involve you, Miss Dearborn."

Annabelle kept her gaze frank and unwavering in spite of her anxiety. She had felt that she and Lord Swain had not been seen together at Lady Locksley's. Heaven forbid if that were wrong! The result would be intolerable.

She swallowed past the knot in her throat. "That is a bold conclusion. Perhaps you might enlighten us further."

"It has to do with a piece of property my fiancé is said to have gifted you with."

Mother's breast rose majestically. "That most certainly is *not* true, and I would thank you not to imply my daughter had anything to do with such an idea."

"The property in question is your own country estate," snapped Miss Abbotsley.

"Precisely. It is ours. That is why this is all nonsense."

"He apparently disposed of the debt upon it."

"Did he? He claimed it cost him nothing."

"So he *did* relieve you of your mortgage."

"Please!" Annabelle stood. Her head throbbed; her heart pounded. "This is quite absurd. Whether he did or did not pay money to cover the debt on Hartleigh, it is done."

Her mother and Miss Abbotsley both looked at her, Miss Abbotsley in surprise and Mother with an expression of stern disapproval.

Annabelle took a breath. "This cannot accomplish anything." She paused, summoned her courage, and faced Miss Abbotsley.

"Miss Abbotsley, perhaps you know that Lord Swain met with a . . . an accident on the road near our house. We took him in when he was injured. He very generously presented us with the note on our property with his thanks. Perhaps you will now explain why you have come to . . . to *interrogate* us in such a way."

Miss Abbotsley regarded her coldly for a moment. Then she looked at Annabelle's mother.

"Mrs. Dearborn, your daughter is just as deliberately misleading me as you have done. Of course it is clear why I have come and what my objections are. But if you must have it stated in words, it is thus: The presentation of Hartleigh to you is now subject to gossip of the meanest kind. It is going about town that there was an *impure relationship* from which he was likely extracting himself, and upon seeing your daughter, it is an easy guess that she is the supposed dalliance. Your attending Lady Locksley's affair last night put fuel to the flames. This must stop."

For a moment Annabelle and her mother only stared at Miss Abbotsley. Annabelle waited to see if the last and most awful accusation came—that of her-

self and Lord Swain being seen in the garden at Lady
Locksley's—but it did not. Then Annabelle spoke.

"Miss Abbotsley, you have now insulted my mother
and myself beyond all which is tolerable. You may ask
Lord Swain yourself about our relationship if you
like, but you will say no more to us. We cannot be
held responsible for what others are saying and surely
cannot impose our will upon them!"

"Annabelle, that is enough!" snapped Mother.
Then, with queenly control, she turned to the visitor.
"Miss Abbotsley, I beg your pardon for my daughter's
behavior, but you can see she is innocent and very
upset. As to the gossip, however, she is right. There is
nothing we can do."

"There is." Miss Abbotsley blinked her cold eyes.
"Return the note for Hartleigh to Lord Swain. Then,
you must leave London and not return."

Mother stiffened her back. "No. We shall not give it
back."

For the first time Miss Abbotsley seemed at a loss.
Annabelle stepped into the breach.

"It is clear you have never been poor," Annabelle
said, "or you would have some understanding of
what you ask." There was a little tremor in her voice,
and she paused to quiet it. "Suffice it to say that I
should not wish it upon you. In any event, however
much we might wish to be free of obligation, we
would be foolish to comply with such a demand."

"I see," Miss Abbotsley said stiffly. "Then you will
allow this horrendous gossip to continue? You will
allow a gentleman of spotless character to be ruined
in this way?"

Annabelle swallowed. "We will, of course, be leaving town shortly. That is the best we can do."

Miss Abbotsley rose. "Very well. Do that, as soon as

may be. I shall be awaiting the news that you are gone."

Annabelle climbed the stairs to her room with one final resolve forming in the battered remnants of her heart. Wager or no, she *would* repay Lord Swain. She would find a way. It was the last thing she could do for him.

Lord Swain did not feel like a hero. He felt like the worst kind of villain in a very bad tale. Somehow by following his conscience—he had, he felt, done that—he had become the brunt of bad gossip by the same society he had done his best never to affront. To make matters worse, his mother was furious with him, and his fiancée was barely speaking to him. In fact, he had not seen her for several days.

As a final dose of salt in the wound, he had been the cause of pain to a woman he would do anything to protect. . . . Well, clearly not anything, for he could not marry her.

And it was not for the reason it once would have been. He had changed. It no longer seemed essential to marry one of his own kind—a woman of similar rank and status, a woman of impeccable decorum in the eyes of the *ton*, and in addition, a woman sufficiently advantaged financially to ensure many future generations of wealthy Swains to come.

He had not forgotten the lessons of his youth nor what he felt he owed his family, but he was no longer struggling with the disaster his father had left him. His mother's money and status in society had been restored; he had reestablished an adequate inheritance for Harry when he reached his majority; and as for himself, he was as well-to-do now as he ever needed to be. He did not need to sacrifice himself for more wealth.

He would marry Annabelle Dearborn tomorrow if he were not engaged to Honoria Abbotsley . . . if Annabelle would have him.

Thus were his thoughts as he stood one evening in the open French window in his comfortable study at Kilburn, staring out at the unusually beautiful sunset beyond his wood. A hawk sailed just above the trees; a soft caressing breeze stroked his brow. He wondered what Annabelle was doing now. He wondered if she was very much relieved to have the mortgage done with and if matters were easier for her. He wondered if she thought about him.

He wondered if she forgave him.

She and her mother had gone all of a sudden only days after the gossip had begun—only days after Lady Locksley's fete. If his guilt for his treatment of Miss Dearborn were not enough, he was beginning to learn that when crossed, Honoria had her revenge, subtle but potent. He was experiencing some of it now.

He sighed. She was to attend dinner tonight. Perhaps they would come to terms then. But perhaps not.

There was one thing that he knew. Matters being as they were, he would feel regret all the days of his life.

The mirror-polished mahogany table was the centerpiece of the elegant room. Surrounded by rich Pompeiian-red walls and windows hung with gold-fringed red brocade, the table rested in its sparkling glory, laid with richly polished silver, creamy porcelain, and fine crystal.

If one were to glance about, one saw, interspersed between silver candle sconces, a solemn parade of gilt-framed portraits hung impressively close upon the walls. Below them one spied a mahogany and satinwood sideboard here, a three-tiered dumbwaiter there, a side table displaying a beautiful ormolu clock in the niche over there. The ceiling was a treasure of ornate plasterwork; and the stately Italian-marble fireplace supported a finely crafted, gilt-framed mirror above, which reflected the glow and sparkle of wood, silver, and glass in double splendor.

Lord Swain hated the room.

It was the most formal room in Kilburn and contained all the memories of all the stiff, silent dinners he had suffered through at his father's table from the time he was old enough to dine there. His taciturn father would be at the head of the table, his mother far at the foot, and he would be positioned near his father's right hand if there were no guests, so his father could utter any convenient criticism that came to mind. But most of all there were the long silences, and the many removes, and the tight, starchy neck cloth he had been required to wear, which made eating difficult at best.

Now that the table was his, matters had improved somewhat, but only to the degree his mother allowed, and for the most part he had supported his mother's dictums regarding decorum. He had, after all, become a rather stiff, formal man himself; it was as if he were proving to his father, two years dead, that he was the most superior kind of gentleman: meticulous, irreproachable, a son of whom any father would be proud.

Lord Swain stared at the beautifully laid table and now saw in its polished surface a strange, convoluted reflection of himself, not the subtly pleasing image of the upright aristocrat he had once imagined. He saw the lonely boy. He saw the angry young man who had taken his drunkard father in hand and turned the family fortunes around. He saw the army officer who had returned from war with scars no one else could see, a man with a new toughness and resolve. He saw the man who could discipline a wayward younger brother but not hear him speak, a man who could dismiss a servant with little thought. He saw the narrow-minded and self-righteous man he had been becoming.

And he saw the man in a simple tunic swinging a scythe in nature's rhythm, hot and tired and destitute, wondering who he was . . . and wondering if, once he knew, he would be able to help his cherished angel, Miss Dearborn.

The truth was that, now that he knew his name, he was no longer the same man. He would never be the same Lord Swain again.

"Is there any matter I should attend to, sir?"

Gregory looked up and saw his fastidious butler in the dining room doorway, holding a silver tray of glittering crystal goblets and gazing at him with mild inquiry.

"No. No, Fines. All is excellent, as usual."

Fines inclined his head. "Thank you, sir."

Fines no sooner exited the room than Lady Swain swept into it. Gregory's mother had a long-suffering look on her face, and Gregory winced inwardly.

"Gregory! There you are. Why are you standing in here like a stock? Your sister and Lord Crowell are in the drawing room, and Miss Abbotsley and Sir Abbotsley will arrive at any moment."

"I shall be there presently."

His mother let out an impatient huff. "I do not understand you anymore, Gregory. You have always been so punctual. You were the one I could always depend upon."

"Mother . . ." Gregory sighed. "You may depend upon me still. As for my sister and her husband, they do not miss my company for a short while. I am certain they have been fully entertained by you."

"Lord Crowell would appreciate your presence."

As to that, Gregory knew the contrary to be true. Crowell was a staid, glum man who much preferred his horses to society. However, Gregory could not contradict his mother.

"I shall come."

They had barely stepped into the hall when a sound came from the main entrance. The Abbotsleys were arriving. Gregory and his mother turned to meet them, his mother's demeanor instantly transformed into one of gracious welcome.

The party soon joined the others in the drawing room. Gregory felt his sister's attention as he walked in, and a glance at her face told him what he suspected: Susan was worried about him, also. It seemed that no matter what he did, or didn't do, others were continually examining him and finding him changed.

"I say," said Harry, standing up from his seat on the sofa, "there you are, Gregory. A pity; now we have an odd number for whist."

"Oh, for shame, Harry," Susan said, flashing a look of sympathy at Gregory. "How can you speak to your brother that way when he has been through such a horrid ordeal?"

Susan, of a kind nature and strong sensibility, did not notice the merry glint in Harry's eyes. Gregory, of course, did.

"I did not realize you had such a taste for whist," Gregory said, knowing very well that Harry did not.

"I shall depart if you wish, and then you may all enjoy yourselves."

"Of course you will not," said Lady Swain, who was just settling into her chair.

"Oh, you must not go!" cried Susan. "Harry did not mean what he said. Harry, tell Gregory that you did not mean it."

Miss Abbotsley sat and regally accepted Gregory's assistance with her shawl. "I do not think Lord Swain is concerned," she said.

"We shall not play whist in any event," said Lady Swain. "Miss Abbotsley, was not the event at Lady Locksley's exceptional? I am sorry I did not go, but by all I hear, it was quite the thing."

A momentary hush fell over the room. Gregory realized belatedly that his mother had not heard the gossip.

"It was as such things are," Miss Abbotsley said. "A crush, and rather uncomfortable. One came from the overwarm house to the outdoors, where it was too cool, and I should not be surprised if many complain of a chill before long. I prefer more formal affairs."

"Oh, I love a garden party," said Susan. She hesitated, glancing at Miss Abbotsley. "That is, I do like the out of doors, but a garden party in the evening . . . with so many guests . . ."

"Susan does not know what she likes," said Harry, now lounging by himself on the sofa and clearly amused. "If the rest of you will comment, she will make up her mind."

Miss Abbotsley abruptly looked up at Gregory, who was still standing by her chair. "Speaking of the garden, let us take a short walk before dinner." She stood.

"Of course."

"Please excuse us," she said, giving her arm to Gregory.

Gregory did not want to walk in the garden, but he knew from experience that Miss Abbotsley was determined to do so. They walked out and soon were descending the shallow steps into the elegant formal grounds behind Kilburn.

"I wished to speak of matters before dinner," she said. "I would like to know why you gave such a valuable gift to this Miss Dearborn."

Gregory sighed inwardly. He had been dreading this talk since the Locksley party, and the time had come.

"She performed a great service for me, as you know," he said.

"But such an act was bound to cause gossip when it came to light, and it has. It was a very injudicious thing to have done. I would not have thought you capable of such behavior."

Miss Abbotsley, of course, was right. He would have readily agreed with her once and joined with her in condemnation of anyone who performed such an act. He even agreed with her now. It had been a very improper thing to do.

"You are correct, of course. My behavior was indecorous."

"Then I cannot understand why you did it. You have never been so impetuous."

He looked at her and caught the full impact of her intent gaze.

"It was not done impetuously," he said. "It was done with intent. I felt my obligation to her. She saved me from a dire fate."

They stopped in the garden path. Miss Abbotsley's face was a pale mask.

"How could you have thought this through? Miss Dearborn is involved in the scandal, as well. Could you have wanted this?" She paused, but not long enough for him to answer. "Clearly Lady Locksley invited Miss Dearborn to the party on the power of her supposed financial recovery, but she will be invited nowhere again. I am certain that Lady Locksley knew nothing of the *means* of Miss Dearborn's recovery before the party, and now the world knows."

"Yes. This is true."

"You must agree, then, that you have made a great error."

Gregory did not answer; he sighed. Miss Abbotsley took that as agreement. She resumed walking, and he kept pace beside her.

"I had thought," she said cooly, "that once Harry's little problem was dealt with, we could consider a wedding date. Now there is this other matter. We must think of what to do to resolve it. But that is enough on the matter for the moment. I am sure it is time for dinner."

Annabelle, her hair covered in a mobcap and a dusty pinafore covering her gown, reached over her head and swatted her dust cloth at a marauding fly. The fly escaped, and she nearly lost her balance and tumbled off the chair onto the drawing room floor. She muttered something unladylike under her breath.

"What, Miss?" asked Bab.

Annabelle shot her a glance. Bab knelt by the fireplace, where she was industriously polishing the andirons and looking at Annabelle with that large-eyed innocent look that was born of a lifetime in the country.

"Nothing. Never mind."

Bab went back to her task and was immediately absorbed in it. Bab was somewhat simple, but she was excellent at uncomplicated household tasks. Cleaning was what she liked to do best.

Annabelle turned back to the painting she was dusting and ran her cloth around the gilt-painted frame. It was a country scene of a cottage in a glen with cattle grazing in the field and hills rising against a setting sun. As a piece it was insignificant art, but she liked it. They did not possess great art, for that matter, nor old ancestral portraits. Mostly the paintings were of the sea and ships, and were purchased by her grandfather. Perhaps this was her favorite because it was of land and spoke of home.

Annabelle sighed. Her arms were tired, but at least the drawing room was nearly done. The furniture was polished until it shone; the dusting was done. Tomorrow she would have Angus, Bab, and Neda roll up the carpet and take it outside for a good beating. She would find another task for herself then, which was not at all difficult seeing that so much had been neglected for so long.

Even Mother was downstairs in the parlor, mending linens. Now that they fully possessed Hartleigh again, she seemed to have come back to life, no longer closing herself off in her rooms. It seemed that Mother now accepted things as they were. However, there was one way that this was heartbreaking.

Mother might be accepting, but Annabelle did not see true happiness in her mother's eyes. Mother had accepted far more than their need to conserve funds and take in boarders. She had accepted the end of her dreams for her own life, and for her daughter's. Annabelle would never return to the world that her mother had left.

Mother also accepted what she had lost. And thus, Annabelle saw her mother truly grieve for the first time—for all those reasons, and yes, for Father.

Annabelle gave a last swipe to the gilt frame and stared unseeing at the picture. Mother had been so happy in London for just that little while. Annabelle remembered the evening at the ill-fated fete when Mother had been in her glory, dressed in a gray silk gown covered in black net, wearing a silver turban with a great black ostrich plume sprouting arrestingly from the front of it, an amethyst broach holding it securely in place. She had moved like a queen and beamed like a young girl—particularly when they had met Captain Carter.

"I met him once before," was all Mother would say when Annabelle asked her about it later—and then Mother's face would assume the mask Annabelle knew too well.

But she had not smiled since that night.

There was a sound at the open doorway, and Annabelle looked to see Lizzie standing there.

"There's a gentleman come to visit," she said. "I showed him into the parlor."

Annabelle got down from the chair. "Who is it? Did Mother wish to see him?"

"Yes, Miss. A Captain Carter. I think she's sweet on 'im! She looked so struck when I told her 'e was here!"

Annabelle's heart dropped like a stone. Why was Captain Carter visiting?

"Lizzie, I do not want to hear such talk from you!" snapped Annabelle. "It is not respectful."

"I'm sorry, Miss."

"Are you not in the kitchen helping Mrs. Bottom with supper?"

"Yes, Miss, I am. Or I was. I am on my way to milk now."

"Oh, is it that time already?" Annabelle glanced out the window. The afternoon light had become slanted and golden, and soon it would begin to fade. "Very well, Lizzie. Thank you for the news. Bab, finish the fireplace, then put on a clean pinafore. And do not forget to wash your hands! You need clean hands to serve supper."

"Miss?" inquired Lizzie.

"What is it?" Annabelle snapped.

Lizzie looked a bit contrite. "I was supposed to tell you that Mrs. Dearborn needs you. She said you was to come down right away."

An invisible band tightened around Annabelle's chest, and her stomach twisted. This could only mean one thing.

Captain Carter meant to propose.

Chapter Sixteen

*A*n honorable man kept his word. Whether or not Miss Dearborn would receive him, she could not fault him on that head. He had unfinished business at Hartleigh.

Lord Swain descended from his carriage in front of Hartleigh and gazed at the modest, comfortable old country house. Oddly, it appealed to him as strongly as before, even after he had been home to grand and stately Kilburn. Here, daily life was ordinary and predictable. Here, the matters to attend to were such as tending the animals, getting milk and making butter, gathering eggs, managing the field work, tending the kitchen garden, preserving food for the winter, brewing ale, planning meals, and feeding the guests. Here there were no politics, no important visitors, no small army of staff to manage, no great expectations. There were privacy and peace—things above any price.

But no, he would not give up what he had . . . save for one reason. He would trade it all for Miss Annabelle Dearborn. He knew that no quaint country estate would give him the peace he craved. It was Annabelle living there that made all the difference.

He signaled the groom to take care of the carriage

and walked up the familiar stone steps. At the top he paused and gazed around one last time. There was the stable, where Annabelle had been keeping the cows by night in hopes of thwarting a thief. There was the little buttery and the henhouse. And the grounds—did his eyes deceive him, or were they remarkably better kept than they had been?

As he was standing there, and old man came out of the stable carrying a scythe. He was small and a little bent, but his steps were strong. As he approached, Gregory recognized him: It was none other than the thief of his clothes, Jamison Kyne. Gregory smiled.

Jamison looked up just then, saw him, and took off his cap.

"G'day, governor. Ain't anybody 't home?"

"I have not summoned anyone yet. I wanted to look about first."

Kyne stopped before him and gazed up into his face. Then, his eyes widened. "I'll be switched. Is that you, Mr. Wakefield?"

"Yes, it is I."

"I wouldn't a known you, dressed all fine and nobby like y' are."

"It seems I am supposed to dress 'all fine and nobby.' I am Lord Swain."

Kyne stared and then he swallowed. "I—I'm sorry, yer lordship. I didn't know. I knew you was a swell dresser, but I . . ." He swallowed again. "I hope ye take pity on an old man, yer lordship, what lost everything he owned. I shouldn'a took your clothes."

Gregory smiled at Kyne. "Do not worry—I am grateful to you. If I had possessed the means to discover who I was earlier, I should have missed something very important."

"Is that so?"

"That is so. Mr. Kyne, are you established here?"

Mr. Kyne straightened and nearly thrust out his chest. "I am. I take care o' this place. All you see is my handiwork. I do the fieldwork, too, and the green garden out back. I got a man under me, too. You remember Angus?"

Gregory nodded. "I do."

"It's a fine life," said Jamison Kyne. "I am a lucky man."

"Yes, my dear sir, you are. I should hope to be as lucky."

"You would?"

"Yes. And now I shouldn't hold you up from your duties. Good day, Mr. Kyne."

"Good day, Mister—er, yer lordship."

Gregory sounded the knocker, amusing himself with the thought that he had actually engaged in conversation with a simple servant and enjoyed it. Once upon a time he would not have given anyone like Mr. Kyne more than a glance and would have been disapproving of any "nobby" person who engaged in more. He did not understand all of the change in him, but he supposed it had to do with having been closer to the heartbeat of life.

He had to knock a second time before the door opened. Before him stood a small, dark-eyed girl he recalled having seen before—Bab, he believed her name was.

She stared up at him as if she had never seen anything quite like him before. There was not the slightest recognition in her eyes.

"I should like to call on the family, if I may." He passed her his card. She stared at it, although he had no doubt it meant nothing to her. At last she looked up again.

"Mrs. Dearborn is in the parlor with a gentl'man."

"I see. Where is Miss Dearborn?"

"She went a-berrying."

"Burying what?"

Bab squinted at him. "She went a-berrying raspberries."

"Oh." He hid a smile. "Well, it seems that everyone is engaged. Is Madame la Comtesse at home?"

"She is." Bab's eyes grew even rounder. "You don't want t' marry *her*, do you?"

"What? Marry her? Of course not. I wish to visit with her."

"Oh. Well, she ain't engaged. Neither is the rest of 'em."

Gregory was on the second flight of stairs when he was compelled to let his laughter go. Somehow his interchange with Bab amused him to an absurd degree, and it was all he could do to control himself before knocking on Madame's door.

The mysterious servant Celeste answered and had the effect of sobering him immediately. He stepped inside into the presence of Madame la Comtesse herself, who was ensconced in her usual chair, again dressed in finery from years ago.

"Ah, there you are, Monsieur. I was beginning to wonder when I should see you again."

Gregory bowed. "I was delayed, and for that I apologize most sincerely."

"It is quite forgiven."

"I have remembered who I am."

"Did you?" She fanned herself languidly with a great fan of ostrich plumes.

"Yes. And I also know who you are, *Lady Ridlington*."

Her eyes widened almost imperceptibly. Then, they narrowed.

"Ah. I wondered if you might determine that."

"I have. And I must confess to consuming curiosity as to why you are here."

Lady Ridlington, the former Madame la Comtesse, sighed. "I did realize that it might come to this. Perhaps I am tired of hiding. Still, I do not wish to be revealed."

"Not unless it is by your wish."

She nodded at him. "Thank you. For you see, I am in hiding from my son. I chose the one place I believed he would not look to find me. My problem has been accessing my funds, which were, of course, watched closely by my son in the event I made a withdrawal. I trusted Mr. Farquhar to help me but had no one to perform the errand for me."

"And why is your son such a source of fear for you?"

Lady Ridlington's eyes took on a hard glint. "Because my only value to him is my money, which he feels he cannot have soon enough. When I determined that he was attempting to have me poisoned, I fled."

"Poisoned?"

"Yes. Poisoned. In his defense, I must say that he attempted to have me committed to a hospital for the insane first, but it proved harder than he anticipated. I do have friends, you see. But he should have won in the end I imagine, and so I was already resolved to flee when the poison was tried."

Even knowing Ridlington's ruthlessness, Gregory was shocked at his mother's account. It was a moment before he recollected himself.

"Ah, your delivery, Lady Ridlington."

"Thank you. It is most kind of you." She accepted the packet. "I shall now pay what I owe to Miss Dearborn. I thank the fates every day for her generous heart."

He felt a pang in his chest. "As do I." He paused. "You need not stay in hiding any longer, Lady Ridlington. Your son has left the country."

"Is that so? And how did this come about?"

"I am afraid I forced him to do so."

She raised her aristocratic chin. "I thought something had occurred regarding my son. I understand that he no longer holds a mortgage on Hartleigh. For what you have done, I thank you from the bottom of my heart."

"Thank you for trusting me, Lady Ridlington."

"Do not thank me. I knew of your character. I admit to a small lie: I *did* know who you were." She smiled. "You are a bit too stiff, and sometimes a tyrant with your family, I understand, but a gentleman of honor through and through. One can do much worse than to trust such a man."

As Gregory left his audience with Lady Ridlington, her final words echoed in his mind.

It was such an ironic twist of fate: The one person whose trust he prized above all would never be able to grant it.

Annabelle did something she never did. She did not go to her mother. She ran away.

Annabelle passed through the kitchen, tied on a clean pinafore, and grabbed her berrying bucket. Then, calling out to Mrs. Bottom that she would gather berries for raspberry tarts, she escaped.

It was a comfortable walk to the spot where the raspberries grew, along a small brook near a grove of beeches. It was long enough for her to reflect on several things. One was that if Captain Carter proposed, she must accept him—but only if she were convinced that this was truly Mother's wish for her to do so. Her fear was that her mother would never utter one word of her true feelings toward Captain Carter to enlighten her daughter.

Second, if she were to make a match with Captain Carter, he must understand that a debt was owed to Lord Swain, and she was obligated to pay it. Lord Swain might protest all he liked, but she would compensate him for the note's value. She would neither have his name sullied by gossip nor suffer injury to her pride.

Resolved, but with a heavy heart, she started gathering the berries. It was too difficult to do the task with gloves on, so she did so bare-handed, regardless of the thorns that occasionally pricked her. For the most part, the berries pulled from the canes easily, and she fell into the rhythm of the task, hearing the muted *tunk-tunk* sound as the berries struck the bottom of the pail, until berry struck berry and there was no sound at all.

Captain Carter seemed a very agreeable man. He was handsome in his way, although his face was toughened by time, and she liked his kind eyes. She liked how he was still fit, not excessively thick around the middle as many men of his age were. She also liked his gallantry to her mother, something Mother had not experienced in too many sad years. Yes, she could do much worse than Captain Carter.

She felt like weeping all the same. It was grief again—grief, her one true companion. Her heart was again broken. She must close another door.

It was not Captain Carter's eyes she saw in her mind. It was the warmth and kindness in a pair of deep brown eyes that melted her heart. It was a touch of tenderness unlike any she had ever felt or would ever feel again. John Wakefield, a man who now inhabited the form of Lord Swain, was forever lost to her.

She stood still, feeling the brush of a cool breeze drying her perspiring brow, hearing the sweet-sounding *switt-witt-witt* of a finch. The beeches rustled, the whispering a rising and falling with the wind. She suddenly felt embraced somehow, held as though by an invisible spirit who murmured comfort into her ear.

Oh Father, if you ever loved me, send me a sign. Just once more, I ask you. Then I swear on your grave I shall heed it.

Annabelle closed her eyes and listened. The finch twittered. The beeches rustled. A man cleared his throat.

"Miss Dearborn?"

Annabelle's eyes snapped open, and she whirled around, dropping the bucket. It landed with a thud, tumbling the raspberries about her feet.

He stood before her, tall, handsome, impeccably clad in fawn trousers and a black coat, which hung unbuttoned to show his biscuit-colored waistcoat. The white cloth at his neck was neatly tied, and it framed a face she saw in her deepest dreams.

His eyes were a deep brown, and the warmth and kindness in them melted her heart.

"Mr.—" She caught herself. "My lord . . ."

My love. She did not know whether to laugh or cry. She had no idea why he was here, and she was afraid to hope for the impossible. But he *was* here—Lord Swain, John Wakefield, by whatever name he called himself, he was here.

He did not answer but held out a paper. Bewildered, she reached out and took it. "What is this?"

"It is a draft from Lady Ridlington for the room and board she owes you."

"From *whom*?"

"I beg your pardon. Madame la Comtesse is Lord Ridlington's mother. It is somewhat of a long story. But she charged me with an errand in London to retrieve some funds for her and wishes to pay you."

"Oh." She gazed at his much-loved face and saw sincerity and some reservation. He was uncomfortable being with her.

She knew now. Nothing had changed. He was only here on an errand. He would not stay. Foolish, foolish heart!

She drew a shaky breath. "Very well." She swallowed. "I do mean to repay you for Hartleigh. This can be the first of it." She held out the draft to him.

He sighed. "Not this discussion again. I cannot take it. Hartleigh did not cost me a farthing."

"It does not matter."

"I will not accept it. That is final."

Finding herself holding out the draft to no avail, she tucked it into her pinafore. "Very well. I shall send it by post."

He did not reply.

She swallowed. "I—I must look a fright."

He smiled. It quite took her breath away. "Yes," he said softly, "but you are a lovely, adorable, courageous fright."

She must have stopped breathing for a moment, for she suddenly realized she was drawing in a great gulp of breath.

"Please, do not." She struggled to regain control of her voice. "Do not tease me. I cannot bear it."

His face immediately went solemn. "I am very sorry. I did not mean to distress you. I—I had need to see you, and I do not quite know how to act. Somehow I can command myself in every other situation, but I am at a loss when I face you."

"You have done it again," she said weakly.

"Blast," he muttered, and turned slightly away, glancing across the meadow. Then, he turned back.

"I have come for advice," he said.

She held up her chin, praying that only she knew how her knees were shaking. "Very well. You may ask for it."

He cleared his throat again. "It seems that an unexpected circumstance has happened. Miss Abbotsley has set me free."

She stared at him, incapable of saying a word.

"I therefore find myself able to make a different choice." He gazed steadily at her, his dark eyes very clear and very intent.

She clasped her arms about herself to stop the shivering. "Well . . . you should be relieved to learn that I do not consider you under obligation. You are free to . . . to find someone of your choosing to marry, someone sufficiently worthy."

"I see." He paused. "Very well. I am under no obligation to you, then."

Silence. Her heart fell to the earth below her feet.

He drew a breath. "There is someone . . . for whom I care very much. The only trouble is that she is much worthier than I am. She may not accept me. I have tarnished my reputation of late, and she may no longer trust me."

It took all of Annabelle's strength to summon her will to speak. "I—I am very sorry."

He sighed. "My dear, *foolish* Miss Dearborn. It is *you*."

She stared. Her heart catapulted and landed somewhere in the region of her stomach and pounded like a legion of drums.

"You cannot mean—" she gasped. "Lord Swain, it is impossible. I am no one. You are an earl. I will bring ruin on your head—"

"I shall hardly be ruined. I am already a gambling cad, and it shall be forgotten in a fortnight."

As an attempt at jest, it failed. Annabelle felt the gulf between them grow wider and deeper, and knew that even if he spoke his heart, his heart would change. Then he would leave her.

She sniffed, and it was a loud sniff.

"My dear girl," he said softly. "I am quite determined on this. It is not an ill-begotten whim of mine. I know myself now better than I ever have—thanks to you."

She turned away and felt the rush of tears come.

"Would you like to know why Miss Abbotsley released me?"

She did not answer. She could not.

"Because I told her how I felt about you, and I told her about my wager with Ridlington. She was quite obligingly unwilling to bond herself to a man lacking in honor, decorum, responsibility, and honesty."

Annabelle did not move. The tears were coursing silently down her face, and to turn about was to reveal them. She did not know what to think, what to do, but she did have her pride.

"Miss Dearborn, *please* turn around."

She hesitated. Then she turned, blindly, despairingly—and found him on his knees at her feet, gazing up at her face. She had never seen such need in his eyes.

"I promise I shall never leave you," he said softly, "not until the day that you bury me in the ground."

He reached out and caught her near hand and brought it to his lips. He kissed her scratched knuckles tenderly and then pressed her hand to his chest. "Even then, my heart will stay with you."

She felt the steady, strong pulse of his heart against the back of her fingertips, and all of her resistance was melting; all of her power to stay aloof and alone was dissolving into a mist.

"I love you, Annabelle," he said. "You have taught me to live. You have taught me what a true and generous heart is. I lived in a prison of my own making, and you broke down the walls. I will not go back to the Lord Swain I once was." He paused. "Please. I need you."

She broke down then, and then she was on her knees in the grass with him, his strong arms wrapped securely around her, and he held her face close to his and whispered soft reassurances and words of love into her ear.

She nestled her face into the crook of his shoulder and his neck. "Are—are you certain?" she asked at last.

"Absolutely certain."

"I have nothing."

"Ah, but you are wrong. You will one day have this excellent property."

She knew he was trying to make her laugh.

"It is little to you."

He drew back from her then and studied her face, his hands lightly holding her shoulders.

"Very well." He released her and drew something from his coat pocket. It was a small paper-wrapped parcel. He unfolded it, then lay its contents in the palm of his hand. "There is this."

She stared. It was Father's ring.

"My ring!" She gazed at it, incredulous, joy bubbling up her throat and floating to the glorious sky. She looked up at his face. "But how?"

"I have my resources."

"It is only garnet."

"No, my love. The jeweler cheated you badly. It is by far the most precious ruby I have ever seen."

He took her hand and slipped the ring on her thumb, the only finger the ring would fit. She gazed at the red glow of the ruby in the sun, overcome with unspeakable joy.

"Oh, but it must have cost you a king's ransom! I am yet in your debt!"

"Not at all. After the jeweler and I had a small discussion, he was happy to give it to me for the price he paid for it. He seemed to determine that he valued his reputation." Lord Swain smiled. "So you see, you are very well-dowered after all."

Her reaction was to throw her arms around his neck and plant a kiss on his cheek. His was to fold his arms about her once more and kiss her in a very different way. It was a way that made all words impossible for some time . . . and Annabelle knew it was the closest thing to heaven she would feel on earth.

Indeed, for the longest time she was lost to her senses except for his tender kiss, the gentle embrace of his strong arms, the golden warmth blossoming within her and glowing in her heart like her most precious ruby in the sun.

Possibly, the kiss might have lasted even longer . . . but for the dampness beneath her knees.

She ended the kiss at last. "My lord—"

"Gregory," he said softly. "That is my name." He planted another soft kiss upon the end of her nose.

"Gregory," she said softly, savoring his name on her lips.

"Hm?"

"I—I am afraid your trousers now have purple knees."

They rose. Annabelle's raspberries were indeed mashed beyond redemption on the ground where they had been. Annabelle's pinafore was impossibly stained, and Gregory's knees sported two great purple spots.

"I do hope your answer is 'yes,'" Gregory said mildly, gazing down at his stained trousers, "or we will have some difficult explaining to do."

Annabelle, gazing at him, giggled, then burst into gales of laughter. His laughter joined hers, and they thoroughly drowned out the finches and the whispering beeches.

Still chuckling, Gregory slipped his arm around her, and they walked home to Hartleigh together.

They entered the house to find Bab busily polishing the candle sconces in the hall. She looked up with round-eyed surprise as they entered.

"Mrs. Dearborn and the gentl'man want to see you," she said to Annabelle. "In the parlor."

Annabelle looked up at Gregory, and he gave her a reassuring smile. "We shall both go."

They proceeded to the parlor then, and the door opened at a touch. Before them stood Mother and Captain Carter in affectionate embrace.

"I beg your pardon—" Gregory said.

Mother pulled away from Captain Carter and looked guiltily around. Her lips parted when she saw them, but no words emerged.

Gregory spoke. "Mrs. Dearborn, I have asked your

daughter to marry me. I hope we may have your blessing."

Mother's jaw dropped even more, and Captain Carter let out a bellow of laughter.

Mother turned to him. "It is not *that* amusing, Charles!"

Captain Carter grinned at her and then at the young couple. "Well, I for one congratulate you! It seems my fiancée was worried for naught. Said she wouldn't marry me unless her daughter did not object."

Mother turned her gaze on Annabelle. "Captain Carter has asked me to marry him," she said, "and I have said yes."

Annabelle blinked. Mother and Captain Carter! Of course! Mother had been his object from the beginning. It was . . . wonderful.

"We knew each other once," Mother said, "before I met your father, Annabelle. I—I was afraid to disobey my parents and marry him." She gazed up at Captain Carter's face. "I was devastated when he left. But Charles taught me one thing: He taught me that one must not deny one's heart. So when I met your father, I was not going to let him go."

Captain Carter cleared his throat. "Let me explain. I had nothing then. Your mother was a beautiful, spirited thing with the world at her feet. I lost my heart but had no hope. So I felt it best to buy my commission and seek my fortune."

"And I let you go."

"And then, when we met again . . . well, I said to myself, 'Carter, you would have given your right arm to court this woman once, but you couldn't. Now you can, and there she is.'"

"He will live here. Is that not wonderful? He has

not bought a place of his own, and here is one waiting for him!" Mother paused, and suddenly her smile vanished. "That is, if you do not mind . . ."

"Oh, no, Mother. I think it is an excellent plan."

"I loved it at first sight," said Captain Carter. "Just like your Mother."

Annabelle smiled. "I am happy for you both."

"As am I," said Gregory. "Now I think we should let you be alone for a bit."

Annabelle slipped out the door with Gregory, her heart full. Mother marrying Captain Carter! And Mother so very happy. Annabelle did not know whether to laugh or cry or to do both at once.

Gregory settled it for her.

"They did not notice our knees," he said.

Annabelle laughed. Then she threw her arms around Gregory's neck and kissed him lightly on the mouth. Gazing up at him, she was rewarded by the glow of love in his eyes.

Thank you, Father, she thought, *for sending the sign.*

Then they kissed again. Safe on her hand where it lay on Gregory's shoulder, Annabelle wore the ruby ring; she could not see it, but for just a moment it glowed more brightly.

Regency Romances From

SANDRA HEATH

*"Ms. Heath delivers a most
pleasing mixture of wit [and]
romance... for Regency
connoisseurs."* —Romantic Times

Easy Conquest	0-451-20448-4
Breaking the Rules	0-451-20269-4
Mistletoe Mischief	0-451-20147-7
Second Thoughts	0-451-20589-8
Lavender Blue	0-451-20858-7